AN IRREGULAR CASTING

A Novel

"A spell omitted from the record continues to cast."
— Pre-Registry proverb, Thornhallow County

PART ONE

The Audit

CHAPTER ONE

The Art of the Residue Lens

The lens had a name. Mira had given it one thirty-one years ago, in the second week of her practitioner training, when her supervisor had handed it to her across a scratched oak desk and said, "Try not to drop it. They're expensive and the Guild is not sympathetic." She had not dropped it. She had instead taken it home that night, wrapped it in a square of clean wool, and placed it in the center of her kitchen table where she could look at it while she ate her dinner. It was a small thing: a cylinder of dense brass about the length of her middle finger, with a lens ground from a compound of calcite and what the training materials called "residue-sensitive mineral aggregate," which was the Guild's way of saying they didn't entirely understand why it worked. It had a slight warmth to it, even in cold rooms. She had called it Prudence.

That had been in the years when she was young enough to name things. She was fifty-four now and had named nothing since, but the name for the lens had stuck, the way the names you give things when you are twenty-three tend to stick.

She set Prudence on the desk beside the morning's intake forms and worked her way through a second cup of tea while Bram Wester arranged himself in the chair opposite, which he did with the careful theatrical energy of a man who believed that how you occupied a space said something important about you. Bram was forty-one and had been her colleague for seven years. He had a Practitioner's license, Tier 3, in good standing, and an extraordinary gift for paperwork that he deployed with a cheerfulness Mira had long ago decided not to find irritating. He was not, by most measures, a talented auditor. He was extremely organized, unfailingly pleasant, and had never in seven years read a residue signature she had not first pointed him toward, like a friendly dog being shown a ball.

"The Pollard audit," he said, placing a folder on the desk with the satisfaction of a man delivering a gift. "Hennie Pollard, licensed baker, Tier 2 Practitioner, registered at the Eastern Guild office. Two commercial enchanted ovens, one proving cupboard, one ice-cooling chest. All equipment listed in the Registry under License 4471-B-Pollard. She's been audited twice before. Both clean. Lovely woman. She brought us spice buns last time."

"I remember the spice buns." Mira took the folder and opened it. The licensing documents were in order: the original practitioner certification, the annual renewal stickers in their correct sequence, the equipment registration forms with the relevant Tier markings. Everything a competent baker with a Tier 2 license should have, arranged neatly and completely. She picked up Prudence and tucked it into her coat pocket. "Let's go see what she's done since."

The Thornhallow Licensing Office occupied the ground floor of a building that had once been a solicitor's chambers, which meant it had an abundance of narrow, dark rooms and not enough windows. Mira's workspace was a desk in the second room, beside a filing cabinet that was slightly too large for the available space and had to be opened at a sideways angle. The front room held Bram's desk, the intake counter, and a display board that the Guild had recently required all provincial offices to maintain, showing the current Tier fee schedule in a font large enough to be read by someone standing in the doorway. The fee schedule was printed on laminated paper in Guild blue and had been updated twice in the past year. Mira had not been involved in the display board. This was correct.

Outside, Thornhallow was doing what it did in early autumn: being pleasant and slightly damp. The market square was underway, and the smell of rain-wet cobblestones competed with the smell of fresh bread from Pollard's Bakehouse two streets over. The bakehouse occupied a wide, low building at the corner of Cooper Lane and Tillman Street, with a window display of loaves, pastries, and a small brass sign that read LICENSED ENCHANTMENT IN USE: TIER 2 PREMISES in the official Guild typeface. The sign was a legal requirement. Most customers, Mira had observed over the years, glanced at it the way they glanced at the small text on a receipt: not because they didn't care, but because they had decided it was someone else's job to care, and that someone was the Licensing Office.

The residue of the town was familiar to her in the way any landscape became familiar after thirty years of walking through it: not consciously attended to but registered, a background texture she processed without thinking. The lamplighter's enchantments on the main street were Tier 1 municipal, running on the nine-year cycle that the town had renewed without fuss for as long as she had been here. The weather-vane on the old guild hall, which had a heat-differential sensing casting dating from before the current Registry's predecessor, still showed true north with the faint amber shimmer of a spell cast before she was born. The market square's permanent stalls had their small household enchantments: a cold-plate on the dairy stall, warmth-retention on the bread carts, the weather-sealing that the flower sellers maintained jointly on their shared canopy. She had audited most of them at least once. Thornhallow was a town that ran on precisely calibrated small magic, and she was the person whose job it was to confirm that the calibration was correct.

That was, in the most literal sense, Mira.

Hennie Pollard was a compact woman in her late sixties with flour on her forearms and the efficiency of someone who had been standing for ten hours a day for forty years and had made peace with this. She greeted them at the back door with the expected air of someone whose audit was scheduled, and showed them through to the kitchen without ceremony.

"Right through here," she said. "Ovens are running, if that's all right. Can't really stop mid-proof."

"That's fine," Mira said. "It's easier to audit an active license."

The kitchen was hot and smelled of yeast and something warm and spiced that Mira could not entirely identify. The two commercial ovens occupied most of the south wall, large iron affairs each standing nearly to shoulder height, with a faint shimmer around their surfaces that Mira's eye caught before she'd even raised Prudence. The shimmer was not visible to most people. It was the edge of the casting residue: the persistent signature left by every spell ever cast within or upon an object, as permanent and specific as a fingerprint. To Mira, residue was simply visible the way color was visible to most people: effortlessly, constantly, a background texture of the world.

She raised Prudence to her eye and looked.

The residue in the ovens came up clear and ordered through the lens: two overlapping layers, both in the pale amber that indicated Tier 1 enchantment work. Temperature regulation and heat distribution were the legitimate commercial applications for Tier 1 in a bakery. Below them, barely visible, was the faintest ghost residue of an older casting, pre-dating the current registration by at least fifteen years. Old heat-binding from a previous owner. Not an active spell. Not Pollard's signature. Mira checked the Registry entry on the form: the old residue was listed in the historical notes column, appropriately identified and filed. Someone in this office, she thought it had been Greaves who retired the year before Bram arrived, had done the original registration properly.

She moved to the proving cupboard. This one had a single residue layer: Tier 2, Pollard's license number clear and distinct in the signature, a gentle warmth-retention enchantment with the characteristic consistency of something that had been cast and then left to run for years without adjustment. Good work. Efficient. Nothing wasteful.

"How long have you had the proving cupboard?" Mira asked.

"Twelve years this winter," Hennie Pollard said. She was watching Mira with the resigned patience of someone who has been audited before and knows that questions are asked and the best policy is to answer them accurately and without elaboration.

"And the cooling chest?"

"Same. Same casting session, same caster. My husband's cousin had a Practitioner's license before the new Tier requirements came in. He's retired now."

Mira made a note. "The Registry shows a Tier 1 license for the cooling. That's consistent with what I'm seeing." She lowered Prudence and turned to look at the chest: a deep iron affair in the corner, its surface faintly misted with the cold it contained. "I'm not seeing any Bond residue, which means no amplification was used. Everything's been cast within the appropriate Tier."

This was what most people didn't realize about magical crime: it was not usually dramatic. The most common violation Mira had seen in thirty-odd years was a Tier 2 caster running a Tier 3 enchantment to save money on subcontracting fees, or a Tier 1 caster whose license had lapsed six months ago and who had simply not gotten around to the renewal paperwork. The system was built on the assumption that most people were neither criminal nor heroic, that they were busy and slightly optimistic about their own compliance, and needed auditing the same way they needed the dentist: regularly, without drama, and with the occasional reminder about the fee schedule.

The Amplification Bond, Law 4 in the formal teaching materials though everyone in the field just called it "running a Bond," was specifically designed to prevent a particular kind of transgression: the Tier 1 caster who needed Tier 2 results and thought they could get there by casting harder. A properly Master-tier licensed caster could bond their power to a lower-tier casting and boost it legitimately, but the Bond left doubled residue, two overlapping license signatures, distinct and readable, and any competent auditor would see it immediately. Mira had seen perhaps a dozen Bonds in her career, all legitimately filed. Hennie Pollard's kitchen was clean.

"Everything's in order," she said. "I'll countersign the annual renewal today. You'll get the sticker from the office in the usual post."

Hennie Pollard exhaled with the microscopic relief of a woman who had known her paperwork was clean but had nonetheless spent the past three days mildly worried about it. "Will you stay for a bun? I've got cardamom ones coming out in about ten minutes."

"I can't," Mira said, and then, because she was fifty-four and not twenty-three, and because cardamom buns were cardamom buns: "I'll take one wrapped, if you're offering."

Bram, who had spent the audit standing near the doorway and writing down everything Mira said, made a small sound of professional satisfaction. He would have the buns. He always had the buns.

They walked back to the office in the kind of easy silence that develops between people who have done something routine together many times. The market square was moving through its middle morning: the produce stalls winding down, the coffee cart doing brisk trade with the kind of people who needed a second coffee at half past ten. A Tier 1 caster from the weather-service cooperative was recalibrating a rain-gauge enchantment on the corner, the residue of the adjustment visible to Mira as a brief silver flicker above the instrument. The caster had a journeyman's badge and the careful movements of someone new to field work. Mira watched him for a moment to check the Tier, Tier 1, correctly so, and then kept walking.

"Did you notice the old binding in the ovens?" Bram asked.

"Historical residue, pre-registration. It's in the notes column."

"I saw Greaves had logged it. Good old Greaves." He paused. "Is it ever strange to you, that we can see it and most people can't?"

"No," Mira said. "It's like asking whether it's strange that some people can tell when bread is properly proved and some can't. It's a trained sensitivity. You could learn more of it than you have, if you practiced."

"I know," Bram said, with the cheerfulness of a man who had accepted his own limitations and found them quite comfortable. "But then I'd be doing your job, and I'm much better at mine."

This was probably true. Bram's job, as it had evolved over seven years, was to manage the office's paperwork, correspondence, and scheduling with a precision that freed Mira to focus entirely on the diagnostic work she was actually good at. The arrangement had not been formally proposed by either of them. It had simply arrived, the way most working relationships arrive: through the gradual, mutual recognition of what the other person was for.

Back at the office, Mira filed the Pollard audit and countersigned the renewal form. The morning's other intake had been quiet: a Tier 1 renewal for a laundry-pressing service on Broad Street, a notification of license transfer for a family enchantment business on the east side with husband-to-daughter succession and correct paperwork, and a query from an apprentice practitioner about the requirements for sitting the Tier 2 certification exam. Bram handled the transfer and the query. Mira reviewed the Tier 1 renewal and found nothing worth concern.

It was, in all the ways she had come to value, a correct morning.

She was writing up her notes from the Pollard audit when Bram knocked on the doorframe (he always knocked, though the door was never closed) and leaned in with a folder.

"I've got the week's scheduling. I was going to do the Merchant's Quarter walk on Thursday, but I thought you might want to take the Veld's instead. It's a full shop audit, Master-level review."

"What's the business?"

"Veld's Enchantments. Mid-range commercial, Cooper Lane district. Cornelius Veld, licensed Practitioner, Tier 3. He's been in business about eleven years. We audited him four years ago, clean file. He's due for a full audit now that he's expanded." Bram set the folder on the desk. "There's a new stockroom registered, and he's taken on an apprentice."

Mira looked at the file. Tier 3 practitioner, commercial license, one registered apprentice, updated equipment inventory with the new stockroom. The scheduling made sense: a new space meant new equipment to verify, and the apprentice registration added another layer of review. It was a substantive audit, three hours perhaps four depending on the complexity of the stock.

"I'll take the Thursday," she said.

Bram smiled, which he did easily and often. "I thought you might. The Merchant's Quarter walk is mostly Tier 1 renewals. Very tidy." He clearly preferred the Tier 1 renewals. Mira did not understand this, but she respected it.

She stayed until four, as she always did on Tuesdays, and then walked home through the market square as the last of the stalls folded down for the day. The brass plate above the Licensing Office door caught the afternoon light as she passed under it: THORNHALLOW PROVINCIAL LICENSING OFFICE, ROYAL GUILD OF LICENSED PRACTITIONERS, AUTHORIZED AUDIT AND RENEWAL STATION. Below it, in smaller text, the operational hours and the Guild seal.

She had walked under that plate approximately two thousand times. She didn't look up at it anymore.

The market square in late afternoon had a different quality from the market square in the morning. The morning was purposeful: arrivals, transactions, the energy of commerce at the beginning of a day. The afternoon was the working-through of what the morning had started, the last of the perishables reduced, the stall-holders making the calculations about what was worth packing and what was worth selling cheap and what was worth leaving for whoever came by last.

She had watched this calculation conducted by the same people in the same stalls for eleven years, and she knew the rhythms of it the way she knew the residue rhythms of a familiar enchanted space: not consciously, but present, the background texture of a life that had been lived in one place long enough to accumulate specificity.

A woman at the flower stall was reducing her late roses. Mira had audited the stall's self-chilling enchantment two springs ago and found it slightly past its optimal calibration, a few degrees warmer than registered, and had issued a maintenance flag that the woman had addressed within the week. She had been selling flowers in the market square for as long as Mira had been in Thornhallow and possibly longer. She did not look up. Mira did not stop. These were the unremarkable transactions of a long-established life in a mid-sized provincial town, and she valued them with the specific, unsentimental appreciation of a person who understood what the alternative looked like.

She thought about cardamom buns and the Veld audit and whether she had remembered to bring in the bin. She did not think about Cornelius Veld keeping one eye on his door throughout the appointment she didn't yet know she'd have. She didn't know about that yet.

She went home and fed the cat she did not technically own but had taken on a provisional basis when her neighbor moved to the capital. She ate her dinner. She put Prudence on its felt square on the hall table, which was where it lived. She did not name anything.

The hall table was a piece of furniture she had brought from her previous accommodation, when she had moved to Thornhallow eleven years ago for the provincial posting. It was a narrow oak piece, unremarkable except that it had been her grandmother's and that she had not been able to bring herself to leave it, which was the kind of decision that was made once and then became the kind of fact about a person that other people did not know. The felt square had been made from a piece of wool blanket. She had cut it to fit. This had been one of the things she did in the first year, the small precise acts of establishing a place as one's own: the felt square, the position of the lamp, the shelf in the kitchen arranged in a sequence that made sense to her. She had done these things and called them settling in and not examined them too carefully.

The provisional cat came through from the kitchen and sat beside the hall table and regarded Prudence with the calm, unsentimental attention of an animal that had decided the lens was neither edible nor interesting but was worth noting.

"That's Prudence," Mira said. The cat regarded her.

She had not named anything in thirty-one years, which was true and also not quite true: she had named nothing she intended to keep. The cat was provisional. The name had been the cat's neighbor's, and would presumably still be the cat's neighbor's when the neighbor returned from the capital, which might be soon or might be a long time.

She went to bed and lay in the darkness of a room where she had lived long enough that the darkness had a specific quality, and she thought about Cornelius Veld's scheduling, and the selenite dust, and the way the cardamom bun had been very good.

It was an entirely correct evening.

CHAPTER TWO

A Very Ordinary Shop

Veld's Enchantments occupied a shopfront on the better end of Cooper Lane, which was itself on the better end of the commercial district. Not the prosperous main thoroughfare where the large licensed enchantment houses had their showroom frontages, but a respectable secondary street where the businesses were established and modestly successful and knew their customer base. The window displayed a selection of household enchantment goods: self-warming bed bricks, self-organizing filing systems, a set of weather-sealed window frames that would presumably stay sealed without the usual autumn maintenance. They were displayed with care. The lettering on the glass was clean. A small sign in the corner read LICENSED PREMISES, TIER 3 PRACTITIONER, in the correct Guild typeface, which told Mira that Cornelius Veld had a solicitor, or at least had read the compliance guidelines, because a remarkable number of practitioners put their signs up in whatever typeface they had to hand and then had to replace them after audit.

She arrived at half past eight, which was when the audit was scheduled. The door was unlocked. A small bell rang as she pushed it open.

The interior was warm and smelled pleasantly of cedar and something slightly mineral, a common side-effect of residue accumulation in working enchantment spaces, not unlike the smell of a library that has had its books handled often. The shelves were well-organized and well-stocked: items grouped by category, labeled in a consistent hand, priced with small tags that were not quite as nice as the printed ones the larger shops used but were neat and legible. A Tier 2 demonstration stand occupied the center of the room, displaying the currently active enchantments on a rotating platform. Everything was registered, she could see at a glance. The residue signatures over each piece were crisp and correctly tiered. Someone ran a tight shop.

She had been in perhaps two hundred working enchantment shops over the course of her career, and they varied considerably in what they communicated about their proprietors. Some were organized for display and treated their stock as a sales proposition. Some were organized for the practitioner's own convenience and treated customers as an interruption to the work. Some were simply disorganized in the way that reflected a person too competent at their actual craft to attend carefully to its presentation.

Veld's communicated something different. It had been organized for use, which meant the organization served both the proprietor and the customer: items where a browser would look for them, but also where a working practitioner who needed to find something quickly could find it. The labeling was consistent and clear. The demonstration stand in the center of the room was positioned to be visible from the door without obstructing movement through the shop. The residue signatures over each piece were, she could see at a glance, properly tiered and recently updated. This was a space that had been thought about. Someone had considered what it was for and arranged it accordingly.

"Miss Ashcroft." A man came through the curtain from the back. He was perhaps sixty, with a round face and a tendency toward careful movements, the kind of person who would describe himself as precise and whose colleagues would probably say something closer to thorough. He was wearing a good-quality apron over his work clothes and carrying a clipboard. "I'm Cornelius Veld. We spoke when you scheduled the appointment."

"Mr. Veld." Mira set her case on the counter and opened it. "I'll need access to the registration files, the inventory ledger for the current year, the equipment log for the new stockroom, and the apprentice registration documentation. If you have those ready we can start with the paperwork."

"They're all here." He placed the clipboard on the counter. It had a cover sheet with a comprehensive index. He had anticipated exactly what she would ask for and prepared it in the correct order. Mira felt the mild professional pleasure of someone who had been brought exactly the right tool.

"Thank you. This is very thorough."

He looked briefly as though she had said something significant, and then rearranged his expression into courtesy. "I've been audited before. I know what's needed."

She went through the documentation while he stood at a respectful distance. The files were exemplary: every piece of equipment registered correctly, the new stockroom documentation complete with floor plan and equipment placement notes, the apprentice registration for one Tam Finch, age 19, Apprentice level, enrolled at the East District trade training center and working two days a week at the shop, properly filed with the Guild and current. The inventory ledger was meticulous. She turned pages, checking entries against the registration forms, and found everything she expected to find.

Until she found what she didn't expect.

"Mr. Veld," she said, without looking up. "Can you tell me about this purchase? Preserved selenite dust, twenty grams, sourced from" she checked the supplier notation "Aldwick Specialty Ingredients, dated three weeks ago. It's logged under 'research materials' in the ledger."

A pause. Not a long one. "Research," he said. "I've been interested in some of the older material preparation techniques. The selenite is used in some historical compound work. The provenance is legitimate. Aldwick is a licensed supplier."

"I can see that." The Aldwick reference was correct; she knew the business, had checked its licensing herself two years ago. She made a note. "Can I ask what specific technique you were researching?"

Another pause. She looked up. He was looking at the ledger, his expression attentive and careful and, she thought, slightly more attentive and careful than the question warranted.

"Some pre-Registry compound preparation methods," he said. "Historical interest, mostly. I write occasionally for the provincial practitioner's newsletter." He smiled, which was a warm smile but landed a fraction of a second late. "Amateur scholarship."

Mira wrote down: selenite dust, 20g, 'research', follow up supplier. She did not know why she wrote 'follow up.' It was not standard procedure. The purchase was from a licensed supplier, logged correctly in the ledger, and the explanation, while vague, was not implausible. Tier 3 practitioners often had interests in historical technique. The compound had no current registered application that she knew of, but that wasn't a violation in itself.

She put a small dot beside the entry. Not a flag. Just a dot.

"I'll need to inspect the stockroom," she said.

The stockroom was at the back of the building, accessed through a door beside the work counter. It was a new space, she could tell from the framing with the plaster still slightly cleaner than the surrounding walls, and it was organized with the same care as the main shop. Labeled shelves. A proper ventilation arrangement for the components that required it. A casting workbench with the appropriate safety markings. She raised Prudence and made a slow circuit of the room.

The residue was clean. Everything she saw had Veld's license signature, all within Tier 3 range, all consistent with the registered uses. The new workbench showed evidence of recent use: a Tier 2 calibration work, something with light-binding, correctly tiered and not alarming.

She was looking at the northwest corner when a sound from the front of the shop reached her: a door opening, a voice. Then a second voice, younger and more anxious, and Cornelius Veld's footsteps moving quickly toward the front.

She found him at the counter when she came back through, talking in a low voice with a young person in an apprentice's training coat. The young person was perhaps nineteen, slight, with the wide-alert look of someone who was trying very hard to be useful and wasn't quite sure how. When Mira appeared, they straightened immediately and gave her the slightly panicked look people gave official visitors when they weren't sure if they'd done anything wrong.

"This is my apprentice," Veld said. "Tam Finch. Tam, this is the auditor from the Licensing Office."

"Miss," said Tam, with the exquisite formality of nineteen confronting fifty-four.

"Mr. Finch." Mira looked at him for a moment, not because she suspected him of anything but because she habitually looked at things. He was nervous in the way young people were nervous around official processes, not in the way people were nervous around official processes when they'd done something about it. She turned back to Veld. "I'll need to see Mr. Finch's training registration and the supervision log."

Veld produced them from the clipboard without hesitation. She checked them while Tam Finch stood very still and tried not to breathe too loudly. Supervision hours correctly logged, training objectives appropriately scoped to Apprentice level, all within the registered parameters. Good record-keeping. Better than most shops with apprentices.

She was almost done when she noticed: Cornelius Veld had, while she was reviewing the apprentice log, drifted very slightly toward the window and was looking at the street. Not obviously. The way a person looked at something when they were trying not to look obvious about looking at it. He turned back when she glanced up, quickly and smoothly, and she thought: either he is waiting for a delivery, or he is waiting for a person.

She made a note of nothing about this. There was nothing to note. A man could glance at his street. She finished the apprentice log review and began the closing documentation.

"Everything appears to be in order," she said. "I'll want to collect a copy of the new stockroom inventory for our files, and I'll need the completed Form 17 for the equipment additions. If you can have those ready for collection tomorrow morning, I'll finalize the audit on our end and issue the renewed certificate."

"Tomorrow morning. Of course." He said it with relief, and then seemed to notice that it was relief and arranged his face into something more neutral. "I'll have everything ready."

"Eight-thirty," she said. "I'll let myself in at the back if the front isn't open."

She had said this because he had showed her the back entrance during the stockroom tour, and because it was a convenience she sometimes offered on return visits. She said it, and he nodded. She gathered her case and left. She walked back up Cooper Lane toward the Licensing Office, thinking about the selenite dust and the way he had looked at the street.

She was not thinking about anything in particular. She was cataloguing, which was what she did. She was very good at it. She did not always know, in the moment, what the catalogue was for.

She had her Thursday lunch with Bram at the small café around the corner from the office, where they reviewed the week's work and ate whatever the daily plate was. She ate her soup and gave a summary of the Veld audit and said, "Everything in order, one follow-up item on a materials purchase, nothing alarming," and she meant it.

She went home and fed the provisional cat and read a chapter of a book about municipal water management that she was reading for reasons she would have had difficulty explaining. She put Prudence on its felt square.

She thought, briefly, about selenite dust.

She went to sleep.

CHAPTER THREE

The Residue That Shouldn't Be

The back entrance to Veld's Enchantments was a narrow door in the alley behind Cooper Lane. It was normally latched from the inside, and Cornelius Veld had told her he would leave it unlatched for her on Friday morning. She tried the handle at twenty past eight and it gave without resistance.

The alley ran behind the east side of Cooper Lane and served the rear deliveries for six establishments: the bakehouse two buildings over, a small printer's, a textile mender's, Veld's, and two more beyond. It smelled of damp stone and last night's rain, which had come through in the small hours and left the cobblestones with the opacity

of wet stone in early autumn. Above the back doors the autumn sky was the specific grey that came before a morning decided what it was going to be, either clear or committed rain, and had not yet chosen. A cat from somewhere was watching her from the top of the yard wall and reconsidering its opinion of her.

The kitchen-and-prep area behind the shop was visible through the internal door. A workbench along the east wall, a shelf of components, the door to the new stockroom. The overhead light was off. The ambient light came from the small window over the bench and it was the type of early morning grey that makes every color slightly wrong.

Mira stood in the back doorway for a moment with the door open behind her, because the thing that told her something was wrong was not a sound or a sight but an absence. There were no sounds at all. A working shop, even before opening, had sounds: movement, the small adjustments of a building occupied by a person, the kettle or the shuffle of paper. There was nothing. And above everything was the faint mineral-warm smell of residue, which was always present in a working space but was, this morning, much stronger than it should have been. Residue that strong indicated a recent casting. A large one.

She did not go in immediately. She stood in the doorway and breathed steadily and thought about the calcite lens in her coat pocket and the form in her case for the finalizing documentation she was here to collect.

The kitchen-and-prep area was wrong in the specific way that spaces were wrong when the person who occupied them was not in them. It was not empty exactly. A space could be empty and correct, a room waiting to be used. This was different. The workbench had the organized stillness of a surface that had been last touched at the end of an ordinary working day, things put away with the small deliberateness of habit: a cloth folded twice, a tool returned to its bracket. A mug on the shelf had been washed and placed upside-down to dry, which was the action of a man who intended to use it again tomorrow. The overhead light was off and the window over the bench threw the early grey of a morning that did not yet know what it was going to become.

The residue smell was wrong. She had been in dozens of working enchantment spaces at this hour of the morning and she knew the quality of it when it had been disturbed recently:

sharper, with the specific mineral edge that fresh casting left, the way a struck bell left sound in the air. This was much stronger than it should have been for a shop not yet open. Much more recent.

Then she went in.

She found him in the main shop, beside the demonstration stand. He was on the floor, which was not how people were meant to be found. She crossed the room in three steps, though she already knew, the way you know things before you know them, and crouched beside him and placed two fingers against his throat, and there was nothing there.

Cornelius Veld had been a careful man, and he was lying carefully, or rather he had fallen carefully, which was not a thing people did deliberately but which was the result of dying with enough specificity that the body found the floor in a particular way. He had been standing beside the demonstration stand. He had fallen toward the window. His hands were partly open. His face was turned toward the street.

She stood up.

She thought: call the Inspector. And then, before that thought had fully completed itself, she was already reaching into her coat pocket for Prudence. She was a Master-tier Auditor, there was residue in this room, and the residue would begin degrading within hours. The Inspector who would arrive was a Journeyman. She was not.

She raised Prudence to her eye.

The residue hit her like a wrong note in a familiar melody.

The first layer was Veld's own signature: his license number, his characteristic Tier 3 pattern, the specific quality of his practitioner's energy that she had catalogued yesterday during the stockroom tour. It was everywhere in the room, as it should be in a working space, layered, aged, and consistent. She had expected this.

She had not expected the second layer.

It was above, over, and through Veld's residue, recent, within the last twelve hours she estimated by the freshness of the color through the lens. It had Veld's license number in it, which made no sense, because the casting that had produced it was not a Tier 3 casting and Veld's license had been operating within Tier 3 range in every way she had examined. Below his number, faint but distinct, doubled over itself in a way she had not seen in thirty years.

A Bond. An Amplification Bond.

Two signatures. One was Veld's. One was not.

She turned slowly, reading the residue's direction. The casting had been focused, not diffuse, not accidental. It had a point of origin and a point of impact and they were precisely aligned with where Cornelius Veld had been standing when he fell. She read the shape of it through the lens, and her hands were very steady and her mind was doing something entirely different from her hands.

The pattern was wrong in three ways at once. First, the Bond itself: a Bond should require the consent and active participation of the amplified caster; it could not legally be used on or through a person without their cooperation. Second, the doubled signature: the second license number was present but partial, which meant the second caster had used Veld's own residue as a carrier, something that was not supposed to be possible with standard Bond technique. Third, and this was the part that made her lower the lens and stand very still for a moment before raising it again: she knew the spell.

She recognized its shape the way she recognized a face she had not seen in thirty years. It was in the movement of the residue, in the cascade structure, in the harmonic of Tier 4 energy running through a Tier 3 frame. She had not seen this spell cast. She had not seen it in the Registry, because it was not in the Registry anymore. She had seen it in a report. She had seen it in a report she had signed.

This was the Severing Cascade.

The Severing Cascade had been Archived thirty years ago. It was illegal to cast. It was nearly impossible to know unless you had trained before the Archival or had accessed materials that were not meant to exist anymore. It had been Archived specifically because, in an uncontrolled setting, it was exceptionally lethal.

Mira lowered Prudence and put it in her pocket.

Her hands were steady. She was a woman who had had steady hands in difficult situations for thirty years. This was a skill, like residue-reading, that she had developed through practice and would have been unable to stop deploying if she'd wanted to.

She crossed to the window and looked at the street. The early morning was going about its business with complete indifference: a milk cart making its way up Cooper Lane, a woman with a basket walking toward the market, two men in aprons from the warehouse district. Nothing on the street had noticed anything. The casting had been contained. Precise. The word that came to her, against her will, was professional.

She turned back to the room and looked at Cornelius Veld, who was careful and dead.

She thought about the two signatures. She thought about the selenite dust in the ledger. She thought about the way he had looked at the street yesterday.

She took out her professional notebook and wrote: *Doubled residue signature. Bond technique. Spell, archived, identity unclear. Secondary license incomplete. Cannot rule out deliberate masking.*

She read what she had written. She put the notebook in her pocket beside Prudence.

Then she took out her communication card and sent a message to the Inspector's office. Inspector Cael Brenn, Magical Crimes Officer, Thornhallow Province. The message was brief and factually accurate: she had arrived to collect documents at Veld's Enchantments, Cooper Lane, and found the proprietor unresponsive and cold. She was waiting on the premises. She would not disturb anything.

She stood in the center of the room and waited, and while she waited she did not look at Cornelius Veld again. She looked at the demonstration stand and the items on it, which had their own residue signatures, all correctly tiered, all registered, all exactly as they had been yesterday, and she thought about what a patient, thorough, excellent auditor Cornelius Veld had been. His paperwork had been immaculate. His apprentice was well-supervised. His shop was clean.

He had known something. She was certain of this the way she was certain of a misfiled license or an overstated Tier, through the accumulation of small details that did not quite sit correctly against one another. He had known something, and he had purchased selenite dust, and he had watched his street, and now he was dead with thirty years of Archived history written in his residue.

She had not told the Inspector what she had seen. This was not a decision she examined too carefully in the moment. It was the kind of not-decision that happened quickly and then sat in the body, very quietly, as if it had always been there.

Inspector Brenn arrived eighteen minutes later.
He was what she expected from the file she had reviewed before calling him: organized, efficient, with the specific attentiveness of a person who had been trained to notice things and had found that noticing things was genuinely satisfying to

him. He came through the front door with his documentation equipment already out and his lens in his breast pocket, which told her he had been thinking about what he was walking into on the way here. A Journeyman lens, standard issue, in a case slightly worn at the corners from regular use. He was not yet thirty-five and had the quality of a young inspector who was good at his job and was beginning to understand the implications of being good at his job, which included the implication that the cases that came to him would, over time, tend toward the difficult.

He looked at the room with the systematic attention of someone conducting the first pass of a scene assessment, and she watched him do it and noted what he saw and what he did not. He saw the body, the positioning, the conditions of the demonstration stand, the state of the room generally. He did not, could not, see what she had seen through Prudence. His lens would show him the surface residue, which was Veld's, which appeared consistent with his registered license. The deeper reading required a different instrument and thirty years of practice she had not mentioned in her message.

CHAPTER FOUR

Inspector Brenn's Very Logical Theory

Inspector Cael Brenn was thirty-three years old and had a Journeyman's license, which was the correct licensing level for a provincial magical crimes officer in a town the size of Thornhallow. He was not unintelligent. He was, in fact, quite good at his job when his job involved license violations, fraudulent registration, unlicensed commercial casting, and the lower-tier offenses that made up the overwhelming majority of magical crime in a mid-sized provincial town. He had good instincts about people. He had a solid understanding of the relevant law.

He did not have a Master Auditor's residue-reading ability, which meant he was operating, in this particular room, with approximately sixty percent of the available information.

Mira stood near the demonstration stand and watched him work. He moved efficiently, taking notes, photographing the room with the Guild-issue documentation equipment. He raised his own lens, a standard Journeyman model, cheaper than Prudence and correspondingly less sensitive, and read the residue. She watched his face while he read it.

He read it for ninety seconds. Then he lowered the lens.

"Practitioner's residue, consistent with the registered license," he said. "Tier 3, which is what he's registered at. Looks like a self-cast." He looked at the body with the careful, professional sadness of someone who had developed a way of looking at bodies that was respectful without being excessive. "Is there anything in his audit file about health issues? Overwork?"

"His audit file is routine," Mira said. "Nothing health-related."

"What about unauthorized casting? Was he operating within his Tier?"

"Within his Tier, yes." This was true. Within the limits of what Brenn could read, Veld's residue was entirely within Tier 3 and appeared to be his own signature. What Brenn could not see, what required a Master Auditor's lens to see, was the second signature beneath it, and the Bond overlay, and the specific shape of a casting that had been removed from the public record three decades ago.

"What brings you here this morning?" Brenn asked. He was not suspicious of her. He was, she recognized, simply doing a thorough job.

"Follow-up document collection. I was here yesterday for the shop audit. Mr. Veld was to have some paperwork ready for me."

Brenn nodded, making a note. "And you entered how?"

"Through the back. He'd left it unlatched for me, as we'd arranged." She showed him the communication card she'd sent him. "I found him within a minute of arriving."

"You didn't disturb anything?"

"No."

He looked at her for a moment with the assessment that people gave when they were deciding whether they believed you and had decided they did but were recording the decision. "Fair enough." He went back to his notes. "My working theory, for the preliminary report, is a self-cast overstep. Tier 3 practitioner attempting a Tier 4 or high Tier 3 casting, possibly under pressure, maybe a commission he didn't have the license for, misfires. It happens. Rare, but it happens."

"He was within his Tier on everything I audited yesterday."

"People do things after the auditor leaves." He said it without emphasis, as a statement of fact rather than an accusation. "I'll pull his recent commission records, see if there's anything that suggests he was taking on work above his level."

Mira looked at the floor. She thought about the second signature in the residue, which was not Veld's. She thought about the shape of the spell. She thought about the way Brenn had just said "self-cast overstep" with the confidence of a man who had found a sensible answer and recognized it.

She thought about the report she had signed thirty years ago.

"That seems reasonable," she said.

This was, she acknowledged to herself, not a complete untruth. It was incomplete. There was a difference.

"The Guild will want a full residue analysis," Brenn said. "I'll request a Master Auditor from the regional office." He was writing this down. "It might take a few days for someone to come out."

"Of course." In a few days the residue would have degraded significantly. Not beyond all reading, but the fine detail, the second signature, the Bond overlay, the specific cascade structure, would be harder to distinguish. She knew this with precision. She knew it the way she knew everything about residue and the lens.

She filed this knowledge. She did not speak it.

"Did he seem distressed? When you were here yesterday?"

"He was cooperative and professional." She considered. "He seemed somewhat preoccupied. He was checking the street occasionally. I attributed it to expecting a delivery."

Brenn noted this. "Any customers, visitors while you were here?"

"His apprentice came in. Tam Finch. The apprentice registration was in order." She gave him Tam's details from her audit notes. She had the notes with her; she had been waiting with them, because she knew he would ask.

Brenn thanked her with the warmth people reserved for someone who had made their paperwork easier. "If you could leave a copy of the audit documentation with me, just for the file, that would be helpful."

"I'll send copies from the Licensing Office today."

She was putting her case back together when the front door opened. A woman came in: late twenties, dark coat, Veld's jaw and something of his careful way of moving. She took in the room in a single rapid assessment, the Inspector, the equipment, Mira, the sheet that had been placed over Cornelius Veld, and her expression did something complicated and then resolved into something very composed.

"Inspector," she said. "I'm Delia Veld. My father's daughter."

"Miss Veld." Brenn crossed to her, making the small practiced adjustments of someone delivering difficult news to someone who had already received it. "I'm very sorry for your loss. Are you all right?"

"I received your message." She stepped into the room with the deliberate quality of someone who has decided not to be stopped. "I'd like to understand the situation."

"We're still in the preliminary stage of assessment."

"The situation regarding the shop," she said precisely. "I'm Journeyman-licensed, and I'm listed as the secondary operator on the business registration. I need to know whether I can legally continue to operate."

She was asking about the shop. Her father was under a sheet four feet away and she was asking about the shop. Mira looked at her with something that was not quite recognition and not quite judgment and was perhaps closer to respect, even if respect was not the most comfortable thing to feel about a young woman in a bereavement.

She was protecting herself. People did, in these moments. What they protected themselves with said something.

"I can't authorize continued operation until the assessment is complete," Brenn said. "A few days. I'll make it as quick as I can."

Delia Veld nodded, absorbing this. Then, almost as an afterthought: "Were you his auditor?"

Mira realized she was being addressed. "I was conducting the routine annual audit. I arrived this morning to collect the final documents."

"His paperwork was always impeccable." She said it flatly, without sentiment, and then looked at her father under the sheet for a moment and looked away. "He took it very seriously."

She was, Mira thought, the kind of person who would be very good at this: managing grief by managing facts, keeping herself functional by staying in the domain of the practical. It was not coldness. It was structure, which was what some people needed when the alternative was coming apart.

“I'll be closing the partnership,” Delia said. “The Haas side. I've already spoken with a solicitor.” She said this in the tone of someone for whom a decision made was a decision settled. "The shop itself. I want to keep the shop. If it's viable."

"That will depend on the assessment of the outstanding commissions and the equipment registry," Mira said. "The Licensing Office will need to formally review the status of the commercial license under succession. I can tell you more once I have the full picture."

Delia nodded. She had, Mira noticed, been watching her with the attention she had observed when Delia first arrived: the rapid, evaluating look of someone who was taking in a room and filing what they found. It was not the look of grief. It was a specific, purposeful observation.

"You were the last person to speak with him," Delia said. "Apart from whoever …" She stopped. "You were here yesterday."

"I was."

"Was he all right? When you were here." She asked it carefully, as though the answer might cost something.

"He was professional and cooperative," Mira said. "His paperwork was the best I'd seen all month."

Delia absorbed this. It was, Mira could see, exactly the right thing to have said: not a reassurance, but a fact, and a fact that was true of her father, and that was what she had asked for.

"It showed," Mira said.

The word hung there for a moment between them, doing more work than a word usually did.

Delia Veld left shortly after, having extracted from Brenn a commitment to notify her within forty-eight hours on the operational status. Brenn watched her go with a thoughtful expression.

"Practical family," he said.

"Yes," Mira said.

She was still gathering her case when the sound of the back door reached them both. Brenn's head came up. A moment later Tam Finch appeared in the doorway between the kitchen and the shop, with his apprentice's coat and the white face of someone who had walked through a back door expecting an ordinary Friday and found something other than ordinary.

"I have a work day today," he said, to the room, to no one. His eyes went to the sheet over Cornelius Veld and did not move from it for several seconds. "I have a key. I came in the back."

"It's all right," Brenn said, moving toward him with the practiced steadiness one brought to managing people in shock. "You're Tam Finch? The apprentice?"

"Yes."

"I need you to wait in the kitchen for a few minutes. Don't touch anything. I'll come speak with you."

Tam nodded, still looking at the sheet, and then tore his gaze away and went back through the doorway. Brenn followed him into the kitchen, where he would take the details: name, license number, scheduled days, when he had last seen Cornelius Veld. Mira had watched this process enough times to know what it looked like.

She had watched this process enough times in her career to know the shape of it: the careful extraction of facts from a person in shock, the slow construction of a timeline from the pieces that shock had scattered. Brenn would be thorough and patient. He was the right person for this part of it.

What she was less certain of was whether he was the right person for the part that came after.

She carried her case toward the front door. She paused at the threshold between the shop floor and the short passage to the back office. It was the same passage that led to the private office where Veld's desk was, and the stockroom beyond that. She did not go through. It was not her scope, and Brenn had not invited her.

She did notice, when she glanced back before stepping out to the street, that she had a clear line of sight through the passage to the private office doorway. The door was ajar, as it had been all morning.

She could also see that the doorway was now empty. Tam Finch had come back from the kitchen and was standing in the passage, one hand on the private office doorframe. He was looking at something on the desk. His back was to her.

She stopped.

A moment later he stepped back from the doorway and turned. When he saw her watching him from the threshold he startled, badly, and then composed himself in the way a nineteen-year-old composed himself when he was frightened, which was to say not very well. His right hand was at his jacket pocket.

He had taken something off the desk. She had no way of knowing what. It might have been nothing. It might have been anything that belonged to him, a personal item he had left there during a previous work day.

She looked at him for one second too long, which was enough for him to know she had noticed. Then she said, "I'm sorry for your loss, Mr. Finch," and went out to the street.

She walked back to the Licensing Office, filed the duplicate audit documents, and told Bram, who had been at the counter when she arrived, that there had been a death and an Inspector was involved. She would explain more when she knew more. Bram looked at her with genuine alarm and then with the steadying instinct of someone who knew when not to ask questions yet. He brought her a cup of tea, which she drank without tasting.

She sat at her desk and thought about Tam Finch's hand going to his jacket pocket, and whether what she had not said to Brenn was professional discretion or something else.

She did not reach a conclusion she liked.

Bram had left a note on her desk when she came back from the Veld shop, which was typical of him: he communicated by notes when he thought the information was important enough to need a record but not important enough to interrupt. The note said the Inspector's office had called to confirm receipt of her duplicate audit documents and that a preliminary review period of forty-eight hours had been requested. Standard procedure for an unexplained death of a licensed practitioner. The note was precise, useful, and written in Bram's extremely organized hand.

She sat with it for a long moment.

Bram's notes were always precise and useful. His notes from client intake were models of condensed accuracy. His scheduling notes anticipated every contingency she might need to know about. For seven years she had received these notes and trusted them completely, and had never thought about what it would mean to be the kind of person who produced them: the kind of person who paid close enough attention to know exactly which information needed to be written down.

She put the note in the Veld file and went back to her audit summary.

CHAPTER FIVE

The Ledger

She brought the audit files home that evening, which was within the regulations: a licensed auditor could retain working materials for up to five days during an active review period. She arranged them on the kitchen table with the precision of a woman who was telling herself she was going to look at them after dinner.

She ate dinner. She looked at them.

The ledger was the center of it. She had already gone through it once, during the audit itself, but she had gone through it with the assumption that she was looking for standard compliance issues: unlicensed equipment, unreported casting, billing discrepancies between the registered Tier and the charged rate. She had been correct and thorough and had found everything she was looking for and one thing she hadn't.

She opened the ledger to the selenite dust entry and sat with it.

Preserved selenite dust. Aldwick Specialty Ingredients. Twenty grams. Logged under 'research materials.' Cornelius Veld had offered her the explanation of historical scholarship, which was a real category of activity that real practitioners engaged in, and which was a perfectly legitimate reason to purchase an unusual ingredient from a legitimate supplier.

It was also the explanation she would give if she had purchased an unusual ingredient for an illegitimate reason and needed a plausible alternative.

She pulled her reference notebook from the case, her own working reference rather than the official records, and turned to the Archived compounds section. She had maintained this section for thirty years as a working record of what she might encounter in audit work: discontinued applications, obsolete formulations, ingredients that had legitimate uses in some contexts and highly problematic uses in others. It was not a secret document. Master-tier Auditors were specifically trained to know what was Archived and why, so that they could identify it if they encountered it in residue.

Preserved selenite dust. She found the entry in three places. Two were standard historical applications, pre-Registry, both now discontinued: a stabilizer in early compound light-work, and a component in an obsolete weather-modification technique. The third was something different.

The third was the Severing Cascade.

She read the notes she had written, in her own hand, thirty-one years ago when she had added this entry to her reference notebook during the Archival training that followed the incident:

Severing Cascade, Archived, Year 34 of the Registry. Tier 4 casting using Tier 3 base. Requires selenite dust (preserved) as primary amplification medium. Effect: targeted severance of the body's residue pathways. Legally discontinued following incident at Guild training facility. Do not catalogue residue if encountered without also notifying senior auditor.

She had updated the note three years later, when she achieved Master certification:

Also notify Guild Archival if encountered. This is extremely rare. If you see this spell's residue, something has gone significantly wrong.

She had been twenty-four when she wrote the first version of this note, and she had meant every word of it with the seriousness of someone who had recently seen what the spell did when it went wrong, and who had recently been asked to sign a report about it.

She read it now as she had read it thirty times before: with the precision of a person reading a document they already knew, checking that the words still meant what they had meant the last time. They did. They were accurate as far as they went. They had always been accurate as far as they went.

She had spent thirty-one years not saying so. The note sat in her reference notebook as a record of what she might encounter in the field, which was its stated purpose, and also as a record of something else, which was its actual one. She had opened the Archived compounds section perhaps a hundred times in the course of professional life: in training conversations, in the rare consultation when a Journeyman flagged something unusual, twice in the past decade as part of the Guild's regional competency review. Each time she had read the entry she had read it with a careful specific neutrality, which was the same neutrality she had deployed when she wrote it.

She looked at the words she had written when she was twenty-four: *Do not catalogue residue if encountered without also notifying senior auditor.*

She had not, at the time of writing this note, considered what it would mean to be the senior auditor.

She closed the notebook and sat for a moment.

Cornelius Veld had purchased twenty grams of preserved selenite dust three weeks ago. He had told her it was for historical scholarship. Either he had been researching the Severing Cascade, or he had been acquiring ingredients to cast it, or someone had supplied him with the ingredient as part of an arrangement she did not yet understand.

She thought about the doubled residue signature. The second license number, partial, beneath his. Someone had used Veld's own casting residue as a carrier for the Severing Cascade, which meant they had his signature, which was impossible to replicate according to Law 6 without either license forgery or license transfer, or they had used an Amplification Bond to fold their casting through his.

She stopped. She went back.

An Amplification Bond, run backward. Not using a Master-tier caster to boost a lower-tier spell, but using a lower-tier caster's residue as a foundation to project a higher-tier casting through. The Bond would fold the Tier 4 casting inside the Tier 3 signature, making it read, at a Journeyman level, as a Tier 3 self-cast. It would only be visible as a Bond at Master Auditor level, and then only if you knew what you were looking at.

This was, she thought, with the cold precision that served her better in these moments than emotion, extraordinary.

It was also something that had required detailed knowledge of Bond technique, of Veld's specific residue signature, and of a spell that had been Archived thirty years ago and was not supposed to exist in anyone's active knowledge.

She got up and went to the high shelf in the study where she kept the files she had brought from her previous position. They were the ones she had not been able to leave behind, not because they were useful but because they were hers. Some things you kept because letting them go would require a decision about what to do with them, and she had not been ready to make that decision in thirty years. The files were in a grey archival box with her old Guild identification number on the spine. She took it down and set it on the desk and stood looking at it for a moment.

Then she left it there and went back to the kitchen, because she was not ready tonight. She knew this about herself with the same precision with which she knew residue signatures: she was not ready, and pushing herself when she was not ready had never produced anything except mistakes. She would be ready when she needed to be.

Her communication card buzzed. She looked at the message.

It was Bram:

Are you all right? I've been thinking about you all evening. Do you need anything?

She looked at the message for a long time. She thought about the archive box in the study and the ledger on the table and the smell of mineral warmth in Veld's shop that morning. She thought about Bram's cheerful patience, the way he always knocked on the doorframe, the way he had brought her tea this afternoon without being asked.

She typed: *Fine, thank you. Long day. I'll explain more tomorrow.* And then, because it was true: *Don't worry.*

She ate the piece of bread and butter she had not had room for at dinner and fed the provisional cat, who had developed an opinion about the hour at which it was fed and was making this opinion known. She looked at the grey archival box through the study doorway.

She did not open it.

Not yet.

CHAPTER SIX

The People Who Loved Him

The informal memorial had been organized by Tam Finch, who had clearly needed something to do with his grief and had responded to this need by sending messages to everyone in Veld's address book and acquiring a large quantity of sandwiches from the market. It was held at the shop on Sunday afternoon, two days after the discovery, while the premises were technically still under the Inspector's review. Brenn had allowed it on the condition that no one disturbed the equipment or the records, and Mira suspected he had allowed it partly because it would give him an opportunity to observe the assembled people without appearing to observe them. He was, in this, not entirely wrong as a strategy.

She had spent part of Sunday morning with the apprentice registry file, which had been a straightforward pull from the office's working records and had not required her to explain her reason for accessing it. Tam Finch, age nineteen, enrolled at the East District trade training center, placed with Veld's Enchantments fourteen months ago following a recommendation from his training supervisor, whose note in the file described him as diligent, perceptive, and somewhat over-invested in outcomes. His examination records were entirely unremarkable in the correct way: a young person proceeding through apprenticeship at the expected pace, without the kind of accelerated advancement that would suggest either exceptional gifts or exceptional pressure.

He had no academic flags. No notes about historical technique interest, which was sometimes a marker in apprentice files: a supervision note about enthusiasm for pre-Registry methods that occasionally indicated a problematic relationship with the standard curriculum. There was nothing of this kind in Finch's file. His interest in the work appeared to be straightforwardly practical: he wanted to be a licensed Practitioner, he was doing what was required to become one, and he appeared to be doing it honestly.

This did not resolve the question of the letter. But it made the letter more likely to mean what it had appeared to mean: not concealment of knowledge, but the protection of a private thing he had loved.

Mira arrived slightly late, which was deliberate. Arriving slightly late to this kind of gathering allowed you to see it already in motion rather than assembling around you, which gave you a better picture of how people arranged themselves naturally. She had learned this early in her auditing career and applied it to everything.

The shop was warm with the compressed warmth of perhaps twenty people in a space designed for ten at most. The demonstration stand had been pushed to the side and covered with a cloth. The sandwiches were on the counter. Tam Finch stood near the door with the specific pallor of a young person in genuine distress who has organized an event partly because organizing feels like control and has now discovered that the event, once organized, still contains all the grief it was organized to address.

Mira took a sandwich she didn't want and made a circuit of the room.

She noted, in the way she noted things:

A man in his late forties, broad-shouldered, wearing a jacket slightly too good for the occasion. The jacket of a man who had dressed up without being sure what he was dressing up for and had erred toward impressive. He was talking to three different people in the space of five minutes, moving through the room with the efficiency of someone managing a meeting, his expression calibrated to a blend of sorrow and pragmatism. He spoke with the two women near the window about the business lease. He spoke with the man from the Merchant's Association about the upcoming quarter's licensing requirements. He spoke with Tam Finch for ninety seconds, patted him on the shoulder, and moved on. This was Petter Haas; she had looked him up in the Registry that morning. Licensed Practitioner, Tier 3, business partner in Veld's Enchantments, on the commercial permit as co-applicant. According to the partnership documents she had reviewed during the audit, he handled the commercial contracting side while Veld managed the shop and craftsmanship.

He had a Tier 3 license and a facility for conversation and was already thinking about the lease.

She noted him and kept circling.

Near the back of the room, mostly separate from the gathering, sat an elderly woman in a good grey coat. She was perhaps seventy, with white hair and the kind of posture that said she had always had it and had stopped thinking about it fifty years ago. She was sitting very still with a cup of tea she appeared not to be drinking. Her face, when Mira was close enough to see it clearly, was expressive in a way that surprised her: this was not the composed presence of a person who was managing their grief for public consumption. This was a person who was, genuinely, sad.

She introduced herself when Mira approached, which Mira had not entirely expected. "Oksana Rael. I was Cornelius's first teacher. He came to me at eighteen for private theory instruction." She paused. "He was one of my most dedicated students. He never lost his enthusiasm for the work."

"Mira Ashcroft," Mira said. "I'm the licensing auditor. I was here on Thursday for the annual review."

"I know who you are." It was said without particular weight, simply as a fact. "Thornhallow is not a large town."

Mira sat down in the adjacent chair because it was there and because sitting beside a seventy-year-old woman at a memorial was a natural thing to do and she wanted a moment to look at Oksana Rael without obviously looking at her. She was, she had established from the provincial directory, a retired Master-tier caster who had relocated to Thornhallow fifteen years ago and was known locally for offering informal theory seminars to promising apprentices. Retired, licensed at Master level, which meant she had a residue signature Mira had not seen in the Registry and would not recognize. And she was Cornelius Veld's first teacher.

"Did you know him well, still?" Mira asked.

"We had dinner every few months. He brought me things for my garden: plants he'd find at the market that he thought I'd like." She looked at the covered demonstration stand. "He had very good instincts about what people would like."

They sat in a brief silence that was comfortable on one side and analytical on the other.

"He must have been a good practitioner," Mira offered.

"Exceptional in his way. Very precise. Very careful." She smiled, which was the genuine smile of someone remembering something good. "He always wanted to understand the theory behind what he was doing. Most practitioners are content to know the method. Cornelius wanted to know why."

Mira thought about the selenite dust and the 'amateur scholarship' explanation. She thought about a man who wanted to understand the theory behind what he was doing and had recently become interested in some pre-Registry compound preparation techniques.

She did not pursue this line. She changed direction. "Did he seem troubled to you, recently? He seemed somewhat preoccupied when I was here Thursday."

Oksana was quiet for a moment. "I hadn't seen him for about six weeks." Another moment. "He cancelled our last dinner. He said he had something he was working through. I didn't press." She looked at her tea. "Perhaps I should have."
Mira looked at the cup of tea Oksana had not been drinking. It was good tea, she could tell from the color and the specific quality of steam that had long since stopped rising from it. Someone had brought it to her, and she had held it without drinking it. That was the detail that sat with Mira after, because it was such a specific, recognizable form of grief: the cup of tea you are given because someone wanted to do something, and a cup of tea was what they had. You hold it because putting it down would be a decision, and you are not currently in the business of decisions.
"He spoke highly of you," Mira said. "His files showed a good professional relationship."
Oksana looked at her. The assessment Mira had done at the memorial, weighing whether this was real or a performance of real, was still present, and she was still not arriving at the answer she expected. What she was arriving at instead was the recognition that the grief in front of her was complicated in the specific way grief was complicated when you were the cause of what you were grieving, and that this was not something she

could see from where she stood. She filed the recognition. She would need to think about it later, when she had more to think about it with.

This was said with the authentic regret of someone who would spend a long time thinking about a choice they'd made. Mira looked at her and thought: either this is real or it is the most complete performance of real I have seen in thirty years of professional assessment, and I am not sure I believe in performances that complete.

She excused herself when the room shifted and found a position near the window where she could see the whole gathering. She made her mental list, which was not a list of suspects, she was not an Inspector and calling it a list of suspects would be to commit to a role she was not yet willing to occupy. It was a list of people with possible access to Archived knowledge.

Oksana Rael. Retired Master-tier caster. First teacher. Knew Cornelius for decades. Had taught him: what, exactly? What does a first teacher teach, and what of that teaching persists?

Petter Haas. Business partner. Tier 3 license. Commercial side of the operation. Had he known about the selenite dust? Did the partnership give him access to the stockroom, the ledger, the details of the audit?

Tam Finch, standing near the door with his pallor and his sandwiches, was twenty percent grief and eighty percent shock. He had clearly adored Cornelius Veld, and was incapable, at this moment, of concealing a thought more complicated than devastation. He also, she noted, was keeping his jacket on in a warm room, and his right hand went to his jacket pocket twice in the twenty minutes she watched him.

A small card on the counter bore the Councilor's formal crest and a message she could read from across the room:

With sincere condolences. Councilor Vanya Bright, Provincial Council for Commerce and Development.

The Councilor had sent flowers, a substantial arrangement, probably from the official florist which meant it had been ordered by an assistant, and had not come. Which told her something, though she was not sure what yet.

Delia Veld arrived at half past three and moved through the room with a composure that was not cold. It was, Mira thought, the composure of someone who was holding themselves together by staying in motion. She spoke to people, accepted condolences, touched Tam's arm briefly in what was clearly acknowledgment rather than comfort. She watched Haas across the room with the kind of watchfulness that people employed when they did not want to speak to someone but could not avoid being in the same space as them.

Mira watched Delia watch Haas, and thought about the shape of that.

She left before the gathering fully wound down. She had what she had come for: she had seen them all in a room together, had seen how they arranged themselves around the grief and around each other, and she had a clearer picture than she'd had yesterday.

She walked home in the low late-afternoon light and made a second, more careful list.

The Councilor's card was the thing she kept returning to on the walk home, and she was not certain why. It was a reasonable thing for the provincial Councilor for Commerce and Development to send a card to the family of a deceased licensed commercial practitioner. The Council had a standing relationship with the Licensing Office on questions of commercial enchantment regulation. A card was courteous and correct and no more significant than that.

What she kept returning to was the flowers.

The arrangement had been substantial. Not the modest expression of administrative condolence, three stems in a paper cone, but a proper florist arrangement, the kind that required an actual order. It had been from the official florist account that the Council used for formal events, which meant it had been ordered by an assistant on a line item, which meant someone had made a decision about the appropriate level of condolence rather than following a form. Someone, either the Councilor or the assistant, had looked at Cornelius Veld's death and decided it warranted a substantial arrangement.

She added *Council commercial contracts* to her list when she got home and looked it up before dinner.

Veld's Enchantments held three commercial contracts with the provincial Council, each running for one year and renewed annually. The contracts were for the enchantment maintenance of three buildings in the administrative quarter: the standard seasonal temperature regulation, the ongoing window-frame weather-sealing, and the periodic calibration of the Council chamber's acoustics enchantment, which had been installed six years ago and required a yearly adjustment from a Tier 3 practitioner. The contracts had been awarded through competitive tendering, properly documented and filed. The rates were not unusual.

She looked at the rates again.

They were not unusual compared to mid-range commercial bids. They were, she calculated from memory against the standard fee schedule, slightly below what a Tier 3 practitioner with Cornelius Veld's experience and record would typically quote. Not significantly below. Not suspiciously below. But below.

Petter Haas had handled the commercial contracting side of the partnership.

She sat with that for a moment and then added a second note: *Haas / Council contract rates: compare to standard schedule.*

And then, because thoroughness was thoroughness: *Who signed the Council contracts on their side? What was the approval chain?*

She did not know, yet, whether this was anything. A contractor pricing slightly below market to maintain a preferred client relationship was not a violation. It was common practice. It was also, she noted carefully, the kind of thing that could make a client disinclined to look too closely at questions of Tier misrepresentation on other contracts, if the underpricing felt like a courtesy and not a negotiation.

She ate dinner and fed the provisional cat and did not sleep particularly well, which had been the situation every night this week and was not improving.

This list was about Archived knowledge. Who had it. How it traveled. What it cost. She put Oksana Rael at the top because of the decades and the teaching and the Master-level license, and because of something she could not quite articulate yet: something in the way Oksana had described Cornelius wanting to understand the theory behind what he was doing, and the way that description had the specific quality of a memory that is trying not to be meaningful.

She walked home and fed the provisional cat and looked at the grey archival box for a long time.

Then she put her hand on the lid and did not lift it, and went to bed.

CHAPTER SEVEN

What He Left on the Desk

Brenn called on Monday morning. He had the preliminary provincial forensic residue report, the standard Journeyman-level analysis from the Guild's regional office, and he was, she understood from his tone, being professionally courteous in sharing it with her. The assigned auditor did not typically have standing in an Inspector's investigation. But she had been there. She had found him. She had provided useful documentation. Brenn was a young man with good instincts about professional relationships, and his instinct here was apparently that Mira Ashcroft was unlikely to cause him problems and might conceivably provide assistance.

This was, from Brenn's perspective, a reasonable assessment. Mira felt something slightly uncharitable about it anyway.

The forensic report confirmed what Brenn's analysis at the scene had concluded: residue consistent with licensed Tier 3 casting, practitioner's signature matching the registered license, no obvious Tier overstep at the readable level, no foreign elements identified. The report's summary section read:

Evidence consistent with accidental self-cast overstep or equipment malfunction. Further investigation may be warranted but standard evidence is not sufficient to establish criminal act at this time.

"I know it's not what you might have hoped for," Brenn said, because he was perceptive enough to hear her silence and compassionate enough to address it.

"It's a thorough preliminary analysis," she said, which was true.

"I'd like your professional opinion, if you're willing. On the scene. I know you walked the room on the morning you found him, and you're a better lens reader than anyone in my office. There are a few details from the forensic team I wanted a second look at."

She was at the shop within twenty minutes.

He took her to Cornelius Veld's work desk, which was in the private office behind the main shop floor, a small room she had not been in during the audit as it had not been in scope. The desk was large and solid and had the organized density of a workspace that was heavily used: a task lamp, a set of reference materials in a standing file, a correspondence box, and in the center, a cleared space that was unmistakably where the most important work happened.

The forensic team had taken their photographs and readings, and left; the room was cleared for review. Brenn stood back and let her work.

She raised Prudence and read the desk.

The surface residue was Veld's: his license signature in multiple layers, most of it routine. The ordinary residue of someone who worked at a desk for eleven years, adjusting enchantments, running calculations, and doing the small precise castings involved in the calibration of commercial work. She read back through the layers: nothing alarming, nothing above Tier 3, nothing she wouldn't expect.

And then, in the right-front corner of the desk, something different.

It was a defensive ward. A personal casting, not the generic defensive wards that came with commercial premises registration, but something specific, something she could read as specific to this caster's training in the way a handwriting is specific to a person. It was a recent casting, within the last week, and it had been cast quickly. Not panicked, but urgent. The residue had the quality of something done by reflex, or by long-established habit invoked in a moment of need.

The ward pattern had a structure she had seen before. She stopped. She looked again.

The ward was compact: a dense, organized structure radiating from a single concentrated point rather than spreading outward from the desk's perimeter. It was this quality that had caught her attention: the compression at the core, the force gathered inward rather than distributed. Most personal wards built by working practitioners were perimeter-first constructions, the kind the Guild's standardized curriculum taught: a frame established at the edges and strengthened toward the center, which produced a more uniform dispersal pattern and was easier to calibrate at Journeyman level. This ward had been built from the inside out. The center was the strongest point. The outer edges, where they met the ambient residue of the room, were precisely tapered, not left soft.

It was the work of someone who had thought carefully about architecture. Someone who had been taught to think about it in a specific way.

She raised Prudence again and looked at the upper corners of the ward structure. There: a secondary reinforcement layer, not part of the central construction but added as a separate casting, integrated with a precision that meant the caster had known exactly where to put it. The corners were the vulnerable points of a compressed-core design, the places where the inward force could leak if the structure was subjected to lateral pressure.

Someone had anticipated this and addressed it. It was not a thing you improvised. It was a thing you had been taught.

She held Prudence very still and looked at it.

She had seen this pattern, or rather this style, this approach to defensive ward architecture, in training materials. Specifically in the historical training documentation she kept in her reference library as a record of pre-standardization casting methodologies: the styles and approaches of the Master-tier casters who had been practicing before the Registry formalizations, whose teaching methods were distinctive enough to be identifiable in the work of their students.

This ward was built in a style she associated with a specific pedagogical tradition. It had certain characteristics: a tight base layer, the defensive structure rising from a compressed core rather than expanding outward from the perimeter, with secondary reinforcement in the upper corners. It was efficient and not common. It was the product of a particular way of being taught to think about defensive architecture, which had not been mainstream since approximately thirty-five years ago.

She could not, standing here now, say with certainty whose teaching it reflected. She needed to go home and look at her reference materials. But she knew, with the certainty of a woman who noticed things, that it was not a generic style. It was a signature of learning, and somewhere in her records she had a document that would help her place it.

She lowered Prudence and made a careful note:

Ward pattern, personal style, compressed-core structure, upper secondary reinforcement. *Pre-standardization methodology, identify tradition.* She drew a small diagram in the margin. She was not a skilled draftsman but she was a precise one.

The diagram was approximate, but it was accurate in the ways that mattered. The compressed core as a circle, the secondary reinforcement in the upper corners as small cross-hatching, the general orientation of the structure relative to the desk. She had made diagrams in her field notes before, for casting patterns that were complex enough to require visual documentation. This was the first time she had diagrammed a defensive ward.
She looked at the diagram. She looked at her reference notes from the previous week's reading, which she had brought with her because she was, fundamentally, a person who brought the relevant materials to a field visit.
The diagram matched. Not approximately. Precisely. The compressed core, the upper reinforcement, the specific ratios of the construction. These were not generic features of the style. They were specific features of how this style had been taught, which was to say they were specific features of how this style had been learned, and the learning had happened under one teacher, and the teacher had been in this shop two weeks before Cornelius Veld died.

"Anything?" Brenn asked. He had been standing near the doorway, giving her room.

"A defensive ward in the corner of the desk. Recent. Personal style." She kept her voice even. "It may not be relevant."

He came over and looked at the corner, raising his own lens. She watched his face as he saw the residue: it was within his reading range, just, and the Journeyman lens would show him a basic casting signature. "That wasn't in the forensic notes."

"They may not have flagged it as significant. It reads as routine Tier 2 defensive casting." Which was accurate. At a Journeyman lens level, it would look like a standard personal ward. "I'm noting it for completeness."

He wrote it down. She appreciated that about him: when she noted something, he wrote it down, which meant he was taking her seriously as a professional observer even if he didn't fully understand why she was noting it.

"The theory is still accidental," he said. "I want to be straightforward with you. The Guild regional office is comfortable with the accidental determination. I'm going to keep the file open for another week, but without something to work toward, it'll likely close as undetermined. With the accidental explanation as the working conclusion."

"I understand," she said.

She said it without inflection, which was a very specific kind of saying something. Brenn looked at her for a moment and seemed to hear the inflection that wasn't there.

She put the communication card down and sat at her desk for a moment. Through the half-open door she could hear Bram in the front room: the small sounds of a working day, a folder being filed, a pen being set down, the auditory texture of a person doing their job with calm competence. She had been listening to these sounds for seven years. They had the quality that very familiar sounds acquired over time: not background noise but a specific kind of presence, the evidence of a life running alongside hers in reliable parallel.

She thought about Petter Haas in a holding facility, which was where he was now and where he would remain until the Guild's enforcement process ran its course. He was guilty of the fraud. The fraud was a real crime with real consequences. He had known what he was doing and had done it anyway, and had made an assessment of risk that had now resolved against him. She did not feel sorry for him.

She did feel something about the possibility that he would be additionally suspected of a murder he had not committed. This was not pity exactly. It was a professional objection to the wrong person being charged with the wrong thing, which was the kind of objection she had always held most firmly because it was the kind of thing that looked, from outside the profession, like excessive scrupulousness, and which was in fact the foundation of the entire enterprise. The point of a fair system was that it was fair consistently, not only when it was convenient.

Haas would have a solicitor. The solicitor would push back. The case against him for the murder was circumstantial, and without the residue evidence she had not yet put on record, the circumstantial case would either hold or fail on its own merits. She needed to make the residue evidence available. She had needed to make it available since Friday morning, which was now two and a half weeks ago.

She got up and went to tell Bram she was going out.

"If you have a professional concern about the residue reading, something in the audit materials, I want to hear it," he said. "I'm not going to close this unless I'm confident."

This was the moment she could have told him. She had the second signature in her notes. She had the identification of the spell. She had the selenite dust in the ledger. She could lay it all out on the desk, now, and Brenn would listen, and he was good enough at his job to take it seriously.

She thought about what "taking it seriously" would mean. An Archived spell. An investigation into who had knowledge of it. The original incident report. Her signature on the original incident report.

"My professional concern," she said carefully, "is the selenite dust in the ledger. I've noted it in my audit documents. It has a connection to some historical casting compounds that I'd like to trace more fully. If you could give me access to the correspondence records, for the audit file, to establish the commercial context of his recent purchases, that would be helpful."

Brenn considered. "The correspondence files are still in evidence. I can have copies sent to your office."

"Thank you."

She walked home from the shop and went directly to her reference library and found the historical training documentation section. She laid out three volumes of pre-standardization methodology on the table. She was looking for the compressed-core defensive ward structure, the upper secondary reinforcement, the specific approach she had diagrammed.

She found it in the second volume.

The methodology was documented under the teaching style of several Master-tier practitioners from the pre-standardization era who had established independent training practices. The compressed-core ward structure was associated most strongly with one specific tradition: a teaching lineage that had been active from approximately forty-five years ago until around twenty years ago, concentrated in the provincial training circuit rather than the Guild's central facilities.

She read the name of the practitioner associated with this teaching style and felt the small cold click of things that fit together.

She sat with that for a long time.

Then she put the books away and made herself dinner and did not sleep particularly well.

CHAPTER EIGHT

The Letter That Wasn't There

The correspondence files arrived from Brenn's office on Tuesday morning, brought by a Guild runner with a covering note that said the materials were provided for audit purposes and should be returned within five working days. She signed for them and sent the runner back with a receipt.

She went through them in order. Cornelius Veld had kept meticulous correspondence records, as she would have expected: files separated by year, then by category including client commissions, supplier communications, regulatory correspondence, and personal. The files for the current year were complete: six months of organized, dated, legible documentation, each piece of correspondence cross-referenced to the relevant entry in his business ledger.

She noticed the gap on the second pass.

It was in the 'regulatory correspondence' file for the current year. Each outgoing letter was logged in the file index at the front: recipient, subject, date sent, date of any reply. The log for the past three months had twelve entries. She checked them against the actual letters in the file.

Eleven letters. Twelve log entries. One entry in the log had no corresponding letter in the file: entry nine, dated six weeks ago, addressed to the

Guild Archival Division, Central Registry, attention: Records Access.

Subject:

Inquiry re: sealed incident report, Year 34 of the Registry.

She looked at the file for a long time. Then she looked at the date again. Six weeks ago. Three weeks before the selenite dust purchase. Three weeks before, by her estimate, whatever had changed in Cornelius Veld's manner enough to make Oksana Rael notice that something was 'wrong with the Oksana situation,' except she didn't know about that yet. She only knew the log entry. She only knew the letter was gone.

She thought about Tam Finch standing in the passage outside the private office on Friday morning, his hand going to his jacket pocket, his startled face when he turned and saw her watching.

She went to find him.

He was at the training center: a low building in the east district where apprentice practitioners attended their formal instruction. She arrived at midmorning, during what appeared to be a break period; she could see young people sitting on the steps with cups of tea. Tam was among them, and he saw her coming from twenty feet away and the expression that crossed his face was the specific expression of someone who had been expecting to be found.

She sat down on the steps beside him because she was fifty-four and had learned that sitting beside people was frequently more productive than standing over them. He looked at his tea.

"The correspondence files came from the Inspector's office," she said. "There's a log entry for an outgoing letter that isn't in the file. The letter is missing."

He was very quiet for a moment.

"I saw you," she said. "Friday morning. In the passage outside the private office, while Inspector Brenn was taking your details in the kitchen. You went back. I was at the threshold and I saw you at the doorway."

He let out a breath that was almost a word and then wasn't. He looked at his tea for another moment. Then: "I came in early. My scheduled day starts at eight. I have a key to the back. I came in the usual way and I could tell something was wrong before I even got through the kitchen because the auditor's case was on the counter and the overhead light was off, which Mr. Veld never did. He was always at the workbench by seven."

"And then?"

"I heard voices in the shop. Your voice. I went through. I saw him." He stopped. His jaw worked. "I saw the Inspector come in shortly after. Someone put me in the kitchen. I sat there for a long time. And I kept thinking about the private office. About whether anyone had been in there yet."

"Why the private office specifically?"

He looked up for the first time. "Because about two weeks ago, Mr. Veld asked me to bring him some materials from the filing cabinet in there. While I was getting them I saw a letter on the desk. It was addressed to the Guild Archival office, and it wasn't sealed. I didn't read it. But I saw the subject line." He looked back down. "He caught me looking and he didn't say anything about it but he was careful for a couple of days after, the way he was careful when something was worrying him. I knew the letter was probably still there. I knew it was about something he hadn't told anyone."

She waited. He pulled at the cuff of his jacket, not quite meeting her eyes.

"About two weeks before he died," he said, "he started having visitors after hours. I knew because I sometimes passed the shop on my way to the training center in the evenings, and twice I saw a light in the back workroom when the front was closed. I didn't think anything of it at first. He occasionally worked late." He paused. "The second time I saw the light I also saw a woman leaving through the front. Older. Maybe seventy. She was wearing a grey coat and she walked quickly, the way a person walks when they know where they're going and are satisfied with something. I didn't recognize her."

"Can you describe her more specifically?"

He thought. "White hair. Good posture. She had books under her arm, the kind with a worn spine like they'd been read many times. I only saw her from behind and then in profile at the corner."

Mira wrote: *Evening visitor, approx 70, grey coat, white hair, books. Twice, approx two weeks before death.* She wrote it carefully, not quickly, so that Tam could not see from the pace of her pen that she already knew whose description this was.

"Did Mr. Veld say anything about the visits?"

"No. I didn't ask, because it wasn't my place. He was a private person and I respected that." A pause. "But he was different afterward. The second time she visited, the next day, he was … I don't know how to describe it. More deliberate. Like he'd made a decision about something and was settling into it. He reorganized the reference shelves in the private office, which he did sometimes when he was working through a problem. He was very quiet."

"When was this, approximately?"

"About three weeks before he died. Maybe slightly less."

Three weeks before his death. Three weeks before his death he had purchased the selenite dust from Aldwick. The same window.

She made a final note and looked at Tam Finch, who was sitting on the training center steps with the careful stillness of someone who had been telling the truth for fifteen minutes and found it unexpectedly exhausting.

"You've been very helpful," she said.

"So when you had the chance, you went and took it."

"I didn't want strangers reading his private correspondence. Whatever he'd been worried about, whatever he was trying to sort out, it was his. He was a private person." He pressed his lips together. "I wasn't thinking clearly. He was dead and someone had taken him away under a sheet and I thought at least I could do that one thing."

She waited.

"I've had it in my coat all week," he said. "I didn't know what to do with it. I didn't open it."

"Do you have it now?"

He reached into his jacket and produced a folded letter, slightly creased from a week of being carried, still sealed. She looked at the seal: intact. He hadn't opened it. She felt something shift, not quite warmth, but the recognition that this young man who had done something procedurally incorrect had done it for recognizable reasons and had told the truth about it when asked.

"I'll need to take this," she said.

"I know." He looked miserable. "Am I in trouble?"

"You should have left it where it was," she said. "That was incorrect. I'm going to take it now, and it will go back into the relevant file, and the most I can say about the next steps is that it depends on what's in it." She looked at him. "Thank you for not opening it."

He nodded, miserably.

She walked back toward Cooper Lane, which was not the most direct route to either the Licensing Office or her home, but which was the route she took. She walked past the front of Veld's Enchantments, which had a TEMPORARILY CLOSED sign in the window and the contained, waiting quality of a building that knows its future is not yet decided.

She found a bench in a small park off the market square and sat down and opened the letter.

It was dated six weeks ago, consistent with the log entry. It was in Cornelius Veld's precise, slightly cramped handwriting.

To the Guild Archival Division, Records Access:

I write to request access to a sealed incident report from Year 34 of the Registry, number IR-34-071. I understand this report is held under Master-tier access restriction and that a formal application is required.

My grounds for requesting access are as follows: I have recently come into possession of information suggesting that the cause attributed in this report may be inaccurate. I am not a legal professional and cannot assess the implications of this, but I believe the Guild should be made aware of this possibility. I am a licensed Practitioner in good standing (License 8832-C-Veld, Tier 3, renewed current year) and I am willing to provide further information in person if the Archival Division wishes to discuss the matter.

The information I have received concerns the casting responsible for the incident. I had occasion recently to hear a description of the event from someone who was present, and certain details they provided are inconsistent with the attributed cause in ways that seem significant.

I would welcome a response at your earliest convenience.

The letter was unsigned. He had not yet sent it. He had written it and left it on his desk, and had been struck down six weeks after writing it, and someone had gone to a great deal of trouble to make it look like a self-cast accident.

She folded the letter and put it in her bag.

IR-34-071. She did not need to look it up. She knew the number the way she knew the number of her own license, because she had looked at it many times in many different mental configurations over thirty years. It was the number of the report from the training incident: the report that had attributed three injuries and one near-fatality to equipment malfunction.

The report she had signed.

She sat on the bench in the park for quite a long time. The provisional cat would need feeding. She did not move.

Someone present at the incident had told Cornelius Veld something: a description, details, something that didn't fit the official account. Someone who had been there. And then Cornelius Veld had written a letter to the Archival Division, and then someone had killed him with a spell that had been used in that original incident.

She knew what she had on her hands. She had known, she admitted to herself, since she had raised Prudence in the shop on Friday morning and recognized a spell she had not seen in thirty years. She had known and had been moving around it, looking at it from different angles, letting the understanding accumulate while the investigation moved in the wrong direction.

She was the only person in Thornhallow who could read the residue with enough precision to prove that Cornelius Veld had been murdered. She was also, by virtue of the report in the grey archival box at home, implicated in the event that had precipitated his death.

She had done what she had done thirty years ago, and she was standing at the edge of having to decide whether she would do it again.

She got up from the bench and walked home.

She told Tam she would handle it. She told Bram tomorrow. She told herself, on the walk home, that she had made no decisions yet, which was true in a technical sense and a lie in every other one.

She opened the grey archival box when she got home. She read the incident report for the first time in ten years. She sat with it at the kitchen table with the letter from the bench folded beside it, and the provisional cat on the chair to her left, and she looked at her own signature at the bottom of the page.

She had signed it. She had been twenty-four. She had believed her supervisor when he said it was cleaner this way. She had believed, or had told herself she believed, that the finding was not entirely incorrect, that the equipment had been a contributing factor, that the caster's role was uncertain.

She had known, at twenty-four, that she was not being entirely honest with herself. She had simply decided that the discomfort of that knowledge was manageable.

It had been manageable. For thirty years it had been manageable.

She closed the file, looked at the kitchen ceiling, and thought about Cornelius Veld, who had wanted to understand the theory behind what he was doing, who had kept finding it, and who had ended up dead in his own shop with his own casting residue wrapped around someone else's crime.

End of the audit, Mira thought. Beginning of something else.

PART TWO

The Archive

CHAPTER NINE

What Mira Signed

She had opened the grey archival box the evening she found Cornelius Veld's letter. She had left it open on the desk in the study while she ate dinner, washed up, and fed the provisional cat. When she came back to the study at nine o'clock and sat down in front of it, she was not pretending anymore that she might not read it tonight.

The box contained seven files. Most were career materials from her years at the Guild's central office: assessment reports, professional development records, the correspondence around her appointment as a senior auditor, the letter confirming her Master certification. These she had been through many times, though not recently. They were the record of a career she was, on balance, proud of. She moved them aside without reading them.

The seventh file was at the bottom of the box. It was thinner than the others. It had no label on the tab because it had never needed one; she had never confused it with anything else. She took it out and opened it on the desk and sat very still for a moment with her hands in her lap.

Guild Incident Report IR-34-071.

It was a standard incident form, the version in use thirty years ago, slightly different in layout from the current one but recognizably the same document. The Guild seal at the top. The reference number. The date of the incident: a Tuesday in early autumn, thirty-one years ago almost exactly. The date of the report: ten days later. The assigned investigator: Senior Auditor Edwyn Foss.

She knew it by heart. She read it anyway.

The incident had occurred at the Guild's Provincial Training Annex, a building she had worked in for her first three years at the organization and which she could still navigate in her sleep: the long tiled corridor, the demonstration hall with its high windows and its permanent smell of residue and chalk dust, the side room where the calibration equipment was stored. The Annex ran training programs for newly licensed practitioners and continuing education for working casters. On the day in question, a Bond Technique Demonstration had been scheduled: an approved curriculum module in which a Master-tier practitioner showed apprentices what Bond residue looked like under various conditions, using a calibration amplifier, a Guild-certified training device that mimicked the conditions of a Bond casting in a controlled setting.

The calibration amplifier had, according to the report, malfunctioned.

The resulting uncontrolled cascade had struck three people in the demonstration hall. Harlen Voss, a first-year apprentice, twenty years old, had suffered severe residue pathway disruption and spent four weeks in the Guild's medical facility. He had recovered but never received his Practitioner's license; the pathway damage was permanent enough that casting at any Tier caused him pain. Petra Neem and Sabel Cross, both journeyman practitioners, had been closer to the exits and received what the report called "minor residue exposure, resolved within three days."

Oksana Rael was listed in the background section. Not as the caster who had been running the demonstration. As the senior observer: a Master-tier practitioner who had been present throughout, at the invitation of the curriculum committee, as part of a peer review process.

Mira looked at Oksana Rael's name in the background section for a long time.

Then she turned to the investigator's summary, which was Edwyn Foss's work, written in his precise bureaucratic prose with its characteristic way of leading with conclusions:

Residue analysis of the demonstration hall indicates patterns consistent with a calibration cascade failure originating in the amplifier unit. The amplifier had been serviced two months prior and was within its operational parameters at last inspection. A contributing factor may have been the ambient residue density in the hall, which was higher than standard due to the concurrent scheduling of two advanced practitioner workshops in adjacent rooms. The hall's ventilation system was not functioning at full capacity on the day in question.

No evidence of deliberate unauthorized casting was found. The incident is attributed to equipment malfunction under aggravated ambient conditions. Recommendations: full review of amplifier maintenance schedule; improved cross-scheduling procedures; upgraded ventilation assessment for demonstration spaces.

The assigned auditor's residue assessment is appended. Assessment conducted by Junior Auditor M. Ashcroft, whose findings are consistent with the above determination.

Mira turned to the appended assessment. It was two pages. It was in her own handwriting, younger and slightly more upright than her current hand. She had been twenty-four. She had had Prudence for fourteen months.

She had written:

Residue patterns across the demonstration hall show a cascade distribution consistent with amplifier malfunction. The primary cascade residue is centered on the amplifier housing, with distribution into the hall space consistent with uncontrolled dispersal. The pattern shows some compressed-core characteristics that are slightly atypical of standard calibration cascade failure, but within the range of variation attributable to the ambient residue conditions noted in Senior Auditor Foss's summary.

She had written "slightly atypical" and "within the range of variation" and had signed it.

She had not, in the appended assessment, written what she had seen when she first raised Prudence in that hall: which was that the compressed-core structure of the residue was not slightly atypical but significantly so, and that it was not consistent with the amplifier housing being the point of origin. The residue had radiated outward from a point approximately four feet from the amplifier, at head height, in the direction of the senior observer's position.

She had not written this because Edwyn Foss had seen her make her notes and had come over and put his hand on her shoulder in the way he had, the comfortable steadying gesture of a man who had been in the organization for thirty years and understood how things worked, and had said: "I know. It's strange. But Ashcroft, the equipment failed. We have the maintenance records, we have the ambient conditions, we have three injured people and no evidence of any individual casting. The alternative would require us to accuse a Master-tier practitioner with an impeccable record of deliberately using a banned spell on a room full of trainees. Which is not a conclusion we can reach on the basis of 'slightly atypical residue patterns.'" He had looked at her with the kind eyes of a genuinely decent man who had just made a calculation and expected her to understand it. "File what you saw. Just file it accurately."

She had not written it because she had been standing in a large institutional space with her supervisor's hand on her shoulder and his voice in her ear. The voice had been measured, kind, and entirely certain of its own reasonableness. Foss was sixty-three years old and had worked for the Guild since he was twenty-five and he had the authority of a person who understood systems: who understood that systems functioned because their participants trusted the assessments that emerged from them, and that a single anomalous reading from a junior auditor could introduce a disruption that, once begun, was very difficult to contain. He had not said any of this to her directly. He had not needed to. She had been twenty-four years old in an institution she had wanted to belong to since she was fifteen, and she had understood perfectly well what was being communicated and had translated it, quickly and cleanly, into the version she could live with: that she was uncertain. That "slightly atypical" was not a lie but a calibration. That there was a difference between what she had seen and what she could prove.

She had not been uncertain. She had been twenty-four.

She had told herself, for the first few years, that the distinction would matter less as time passed. It had not mattered less. It had simply become a fixed point, a thing that was true and had always been true and that she had organized her professional life around not looking at directly, the way you organized your route through a room around a piece of furniture that was slightly in the wrong place. You learned the correct path. You stopped noticing you were taking it.

She had. She had filed it accurately in the sense that "slightly atypical" was a more cautious version of what she had seen, and "within the range of variation" was a phrase designed to close a door without locking it. She had been junior, and Foss had been senior, and Foss had been kind. The Guild was large, and she had been twenty-four.

At the bottom of the second page of her appended assessment: her signature. M. Ashcroft, Junior Auditor, Master Candidacy Year 2.

She had not forgotten her own handwriting. She had not forgotten what it had felt like to form those letters: the careful deliberateness of someone writing something they were not entirely sure they believed.

She had been twenty-four and she had formed those letters and she had believed, at the time of forming them, that she was doing the most defensible thing available to her in a situation that offered few defensible options. This was not entirely wrong. She had also believed, at twenty-four, that the version of herself who was fifty-four would have resolved the distinction between defensible and correct into something she could live with more comfortably.

She had not. She had lived with it the way most people lived with the things they had not resolved: by not looking directly at them, by organizing the rest of her life in such a way that the looking was never strictly required. This had been possible because Edwyn Foss had retired to his garden and never revisited the file. Oksana Rael had gone quietly to Thornhallow. The incident report had sat in its sealed file. No one had been badly harmed by the looking-away, or so she had told herself, which was the other thing she had lived with.

Harlen Voss was in his early fifties and ran a plant nursery. She had looked him up six months after she achieved her Master certification, at which point she could have amended the assessment, and had found that he was alive and had made a life and that the life was apparently not entirely defined by what had happened to him when he was twenty. She had filed this as evidence that the looking-away had not been a catastrophe. She understood now that this was one of the less defensible things she had told herself.

She turned back to the main report. Oksana Rael, senior observer. Present throughout.

She had demonstrated Bond technique, Mira now understood, in exactly the way the curriculum called for. She had stood at the front of the room and conducted the session while the calibration amplifier hummed on its stand. And at some point during the demonstration she had cast the Severing Cascade not through the amplifier, which would have registered clearly on any lens, but through a Bond folded into the ambient residue of the room itself, which was what had produced the compressed-core distribution Mira had seen: the cascade had originated from a point in space, not from a device, because it had originated from a person.

The amplifier had been the misdirection. The ambient residue conditions had been the cover. And a young apprentice named Harlen Voss had been standing in exactly the wrong place.

She did not know why. Thirty years later, she still did not know why. That was the part that had always been the most difficult to sit with: the absence of a motive she could understand. Oksana Rael had nothing against Harlen Voss. He was nobody to her. Which meant either that the wrong person had been struck and someone else was the target, or that the Severing Cascade had been cast not to harm anyone specifically but to demonstrate something: to practice the technique, perhaps, under real conditions, using real residue and real ambient cover, to see if it could be done without detection.

To see if it could be done without detection.

She sat with that.

Then she closed the file and put it back in the grey archival box and put the box on the high shelf.

She opened it again twenty minutes later and took the file back out.

She read the name in the background section once more: Oksana Rael, senior observer. Present throughout.

Then she closed the file and this time left it closed.

CHAPTER TEN

Petter Haas's Alibi Has a Hole in It

On Tuesday morning, Bram had a scheduling conflict with the Merchant's Quarter walk-through and came to Mira's desk with two cups of tea and the expression of a man who had something administrative to raise and was going to raise it pleasantly regardless of her mood.

"I've been through the Veld file index," he said. "The predecessor file, the one from the audit four years ago." He set a tea in front of her. "There are some notes in there from the previous auditor that aren't in the current working file. I think they got separated during the reorganization when we changed the filing system."

She looked at him. "What kind of notes?"

"Mostly routine. But there's a note in the margins of the equipment registration from four years ago that says," he consulted his folder, "cross-reference partnership agreements for commercial contract amendments. In pencil. The previous auditor's handwriting, not a formal notation."

She looked at the note when Bram set it in front of her. Greaves, whom she had known briefly before his retirement, had written it beside the commercial license renewal: *x-ref partnership agmts for comm. contract amends.* A reminder to himself, or a flag for the next audit. A thing he had noticed and intended to follow up.

She thought about Haas's commercial contracting records. She thought about the Council contracts and the rates slightly below standard.

"Thank you," she said. "Leave it with me."

Bram nodded, with the cheerfulness of a man who had done a useful thing and found that adequate. He picked up his own tea and went back to the front room. She sat for a moment with the penciled note and the faint echo of a colleague who had noticed something four years ago, who had filed it as a future task, and who had then retired before the future task arrived.

She added it to her working file and found that it sat exactly where she had expected it to sit: beside the audit entries for the commercial contracts, which were Haas's side of the partnership, and which she had not yet gone through as carefully as she was about to.

She had found the gap in Haas's alibi not by looking for it but by doing what she always did: reading the edges of things carefully. The partnership documents she had reviewed during the audit included the contracts for the current year's major commissions, and one of those contracts had a start date that conflicted with the supplier meeting Haas had claimed as his alibi for Friday morning.

She brought this to Brenn on Wednesday, five days after finding Cornelius Veld. She brought it as a question, professionally phrased, about whether the timeline of the partnership's largest current commission was relevant to the investigation, and she let Brenn work out the implication himself, which he did within three minutes.

"He said he was at a supplier meeting in the Merchant's Quarter from seven to noon."

"The commission contract starts on the fifteenth," Mira said. "The contract specifies that all supplier meetings for the project are to occur after the project start date, to ensure licensing compliance. The fifteenth is next week."

Brenn looked at the contract for a long moment. Then he looked at the supplier contact information.

"I'll check," he said.

The supplier confirmed the meeting: it had happened, Haas had been there, and it had concluded by half past nine, not noon as Haas had claimed. A gap of an hour and a half, unaccounted for, on the morning of Cornelius Veld's death.

This was, she could see from Brenn's expression when he called to tell her, significant. He had the gap, he had the motive question, and he had begun pulling the commission records she had mentioned. What he found when he pulled them was, she suspected, more interesting than the alibi gap.

She asked him if he had looked at the Tier declarations on the commercial contracts.

A pause. "What am I looking for?"

"Cross-reference the Tier billed on each contract against the registered Tier for the work described. Specifically the weather-proofing commissions from the past two years."

Another pause. Longer.

"He's billing Tier 4 rates," Brenn said.

"For Tier 3 work, yes. He's been representing his services as within the Tier 4 range on the commercial contracts. The actual work is within his Tier 3 license." She waited a moment. "Cornelius Veld knew. He would have seen it in the billing records. He was, by his own account in the partnership agreement, the one who reviewed the annual accounts."

"And he was about to dissolve the partnership," Brenn said slowly, working backward through what this meant.

"According to the correspondence I reviewed during the audit, yes. There's a letter from a solicitor dated six weeks ago, advising Mr. Veld on the dissolution process."

Brenn was quiet for a moment. She could hear him thinking, the precise and careful thinking of a person who was assembling something and wanted to be sure the pieces fit before he said so.

"You held this back," he said. Not an accusation. An observation.

"I was completing the audit. The licensing violation is a separate matter from the investigation."

"But you knew it was relevant."

"I knew it was potentially relevant," she said, which was slightly different and also the best she could honestly offer.

Another pause. "All right," he said. "I appreciate you bringing it to me now."

She put the communication card down and sat at her desk for a moment.

It was a very good case against Petter Haas. He had motive, the partnership dissolution and the fraud Cornelius was about to expose. He had a plausible means, access to the shop through the partnership. He had an alibi that didn't hold for ninety minutes on the morning of the death. He had a character consistent with a man who made quiet, profitable, self-serving decisions and was not especially troubled by the rules he bent in making them.

She sat with the case against Haas for the better part of an afternoon, which was the honest version of what due diligence required: not moving past a compelling theory because a different theory was available, but testing the compelling theory against everything she had and finding out where it broke.

She started from the fraud. Petter Haas had been billing Tier 4 rates on Tier 3 work for at least two years, possibly longer. The commercial contracts were his side of the partnership. Cornelius Veld reviewed the annual accounts. Veld had recently engaged a solicitor regarding the dissolution of the partnership. A man who had been running a billing fraud and was about to be exposed by his business partner had a clear and comprehensible motive for wanting that partner not to report him to the Guild. The financial penalty for category-two misrepresentation was significant. The reputational penalty was worse. The licensing implications, in a jurisdiction that required Tier endorsement for commercial contracts, could effectively end a career.

All of this was real. She wrote it down in her working notes and underlined it.

Then she wrote, on the next line: *Severing Cascade. Inverted Bond technique. Archived Tier 4. Pre-Registry compound formulation.*

She stared at these two lists for a long time.

The gap between them was not a matter of motive. It was a matter of knowledge. A commercial weather-proofer who had been to the Guild's southern circuit training facility in the late years of the previous Registry period had no pathway to the specific, Archived, historically obscure technique that had killed Cornelius Veld. Unless he had been introduced to it. Unless someone had sold him access to it.

She thought about Oksana Rael's underground network of Archived knowledge, which she had been piecing together from the supplier records and the licensing database and the pattern of procurement. She thought about whether Haas could have been a client of that network. She thought about whether a man who misrepresented his Tier on commercial contracts was also the kind of man who purchased Archived spell knowledge from a retired Master-tier caster through informal channels.

She could not rule it out entirely. He was the kind of person who, if such a thing were available and profitable, might find it interesting. But the nature of the purchase was different. Billing fraud was self-serving in the most direct possible way: more money, less effort, in a domain where the odds of detection were low. Archived spell knowledge had no obvious commercial application for a weather-proofer. There was no way to bill Tier 4 rates for a Severing Cascade without also explaining to your client why their business partner was dead in a way that made you immediately the primary suspect.

The fraud was practical. The murder was something else entirely. And Mira had spent thirty years learning to read the difference.

What he did not have was any conceivable connection to the Severing Cascade.

She tried, because thoroughness required it.

She pulled Haas's licensing history from the Guild's regional records: a standard progression, Tier 1 provisional at twenty-two, Tier 2 certification at twenty-five, Tier 3 commercial endorsement three years later. His training institution was the Guild's southern circuit facility, a large, well-resourced program that had produced more competent commercial practitioners than perhaps any other training center in the province. His training records, which she had limited access to but could review in summary, showed a standard curriculum: the core commercial enchantment subjects, the business practice modules, the regulatory compliance training that had been mandatory since Year 28 of the Registry.

Nothing unusual. No electives in historical technique. No notation of archival interest. No association with any practitioner known to the informal knowledge trade that she had been piecing together over the past two weeks.

She thought about what the Severing Cascade required: not just the technical knowledge, which was genuinely obscure, but the specific Bond technique to mask the second signature, which required a level of sophistication that could not be self-taught from archived descriptions. It required someone who had been taught by someone who had known the technique before the Archival, or who had acquired it through the informal network Oksana ran.

Petter Haas was not that kind of person. Not because he was incapable of the fraud, which he was clearly capable of; but because the fraud and the magic were different categories of transgression. The fraud was practical and self-serving, and operated within the logic of commercial advantage. The Severing Cascade required a different kind of knowledge, a different kind of relationship to the rules, a different kind of person.

She filed this. It was not proof. It was a professional judgment about character and it could be wrong. But she had been reading professional character in the residue of people's work for thirty years, and she had developed a reliable sense of the specific shape that different kinds of transgression left behind. Haas had the shape of a man who cheated the billing system. The Severing Cascade had been cast by someone with an entirely different relationship to the rules: someone who had spent decades deciding which rules were real and which were merely administrative, and who had acted accordingly.

Petter Haas was a commercial contractor. His Tier 3 license was in weather-proofing, industrial heat enchantment, and structural-stability spellwork. His entire career was in the practical application of mid-level commercial magic. The Severing Cascade was an Archived Tier 4 casting using a Bond technique that required not only Master-level knowledge but knowledge of a specific historical formulation that had been removed from all public training materials thirty years ago. A man who billed Tier 3 work at Tier 4 rates did not have access to a spell that had been officially erased from existence before he would have completed his journeyman training.

She could not reconcile these two things. She had been trying to reconcile them since she first read the alibi discrepancy, and the reconciliation was not there.

There were three possible explanations. First: Haas had somehow acquired knowledge of the Archived spell through means she had not yet uncovered, and had the motive and means she had already documented, and the alibi gap was what it looked like. Second: Haas was innocent of the murder but guilty of the fraud and the alibi fabrication, and someone else had used the ninety-minute gap as a convenient coincidence. Third: the alibi gap and the fraud were unrelated to the death, the accidental determination was correct, and she had been wrong about the residue.

She did not believe the third explanation. She had not been wrong about residue in thirty years.

She did not have enough to argue for the second against a solid working theory.

She had, and this was the precise location of the problem, one piece of evidence that would resolve it: the residue reading she had taken on Friday morning, with Prudence, before she called Inspector Brenn. She had not shared this. She still had not shared it. The argument for sharing it now was clear: it would redirect the investigation. The argument against sharing it was that the moment she put a doubled signature and a Severing Cascade on record, someone would want to know about the Archived spell. The Archived spell would lead to the original incident. The original incident led to IR-34-071, and to her signature at the bottom of the appended assessment.

She knew the shape of what she was doing. She had known it since the morning she stood in Veld's shop and let Brenn conclude self-cast overstep. She was conflict-avoidant and she was sixty-nine steps ahead of the consequences and both of these things were, she was prepared to admit, problems.

She thought about Petter Haas, who was genuinely guilty of things. She thought about the license fraud, which was real and provable, and would result in a significant penalty. She thought about the partnership deception, which was also real. She thought about what it would mean for a man who had done these things to be investigated for a murder he had almost certainly not committed.

This was, she decided, not entirely a satisfying avenue of thought.

She went back to her audit files and began making a list of Master-tier casters in the province who might have knowledge of pre-Archival technique. It was a short list and it kept narrowing toward the same name, and she kept writing around the name until there was nowhere left to write.

She went to the Merchant's Quarter on Wednesday morning, which was not a scheduled audit day and which she described to Bram, accurately if incompletely, as a follow-up walk.

The Merchant's Quarter in the morning had the efficiency of a district that ran on commercial time: deliveries before nine, the shops open by half past, the middle morning occupied with the specific transactions that made the district function. She was not here to audit. She was here to place a man in space and time on a Friday morning three weeks ago.

The coffee cart on the south corner of the Quarter was one of five establishments she had identified as likely to be open before eight on a weekday morning. She went to the south corner first because it was the corner closest to both the supplier meeting location Haas had given Brenn and the route from that location to Cooper Lane.

The woman operating the cart was in her forties and had the specific memory of someone whose livelihood involved recognizing repeat customers. "Three weeks ago Friday," Mira said, and gave the date. "A man, late forties, broad-shouldered. Would have been here between eight and ten in the morning, possibly twice. He might have been moving quickly, or standing, waiting."

The woman thought. She pulled three cups of coffee in the interval of thinking. "Big coat? Nicely dressed?"

"That's possible."

"I had someone standing on the corner for about twenty minutes that morning. Around half past eight. He had a coffee, just the one, and he kept looking toward the lane." She shrugged. "I assumed he was waiting for someone. Men do that. Stand on corners waiting for someone and then not meet anyone."

"Did he go toward the lane, eventually?"

"I don't know. I got busy. He was gone when I looked again."

Mira thanked her and walked toward Cooper Lane herself, not quickly. Twenty minutes at the corner from half past eight. That put Haas, if it had been Haas, within four minutes' walk of Veld's Enchantments between eight-thirty and nine. The front entrance was unlocked after eight; Veld had been an early opener. The back entrance was the one she had used herself. She stood in the alley behind Cooper Lane and thought about this.

The description was not specific enough to be certain. A broad-shouldered man in a good coat standing on a commercial street corner on a weekday morning could have been Haas or could have been half a dozen other people. The coffee cart woman's estimate of twenty minutes was approximate. The fact of a man watching a lane and then being gone proved nothing about where he had gone.

What she found, when she raised Prudence and read the residue in the alley itself, was more informative.

There was nothing to find. The alley had the residue footprint of a working commercial district: ambient Tier 1 and Tier 2 from the surrounding shops, the faint historical deposit of decades of licensed commercial activity. No fresh residue. No Tier 3 signature. No Bond overlay or traces of anything that would suggest a commercial contractor with Haas's specific license pattern had been standing here recently.

She lowered the lens.

A man of Haas's practical commercial experience did not cast spells on morning walks. He was a weather-proofer, an industrial heat enchanter, a structural-stability caster. He would not produce casting residue in an alley simply by walking through it.

But neither would someone skilled enough to mask a murder in Bond technique.

She put Prudence back in her pocket and walked back through the Merchant's Quarter in the direction of the Licensing Office. She thought about two things that were both true but did not fit together, and about what it meant that they didn't.

CHAPTER ELEVEN

Oksana Rael Takes Tea

She went to Oksana on a Thursday, which was not one of her office days, and she went in the morning because Oksana's informal theory seminars ran on Thursday afternoons and Mira wanted to find her at home and unhurried. She had a pretext ready: she was compiling notes for a professional development piece on Bond technique applications for the Guild's regional newsletter, which she did occasionally contribute to and which Oksana would know. It was thin. It was thin the way all pretexts were thin to the people who invented them and opaque to everyone else.

Oksana lived on Rael Street, which was named for an ancestor and amused her, she had mentioned once, precisely because she had had nothing to do with the naming. The house was mid-terrace, stone-fronted, with a garden in the back that was audible from the street: the alive-sound of a garden that was actively maintained and not merely existing. A knocker in the shape of a calibration wrench, which was a Guild in-joke from forty years ago, still current if you knew the reference.

Oksana opened the door herself. She was wearing a work apron over her clothes, which meant she had been in the garden. She looked at Mira for one beat before her expression settled into something warm and welcoming, and Mira filed the beat without letting on she had noticed it.

"Miss Ashcroft. Come in. I've just put the kettle on."

The interior of the house had the comfortable density of someone who had lived in a space for fifteen years and had made it entirely their own. Bookshelves in the sitting room, floor to ceiling on two walls. A worktable near the window with the organized disorder of active theoretical work: papers, reference volumes, a residue observation journal of the kind that Master-tier casters kept for their own professional records. Mira noted the title of one of the visible reference volumes: a pre-standardization compendium of casting methodologies, third edition, well-thumbed.

She sat down in the offered chair, which was comfortable and positioned with its back to the window, which put her face in shadow and Oksana's in light. She was not sure whether this was deliberate. It was the kind of thing that might be or might not be, and the uncertainty was itself informative.

Tea arrived with the efficiency of a woman who knew where everything in her kitchen was. It was very good tea, the kind that came from somewhere specific and was bought on purpose.

"You said you were working on a piece about Bond technique," Oksana said, settling into the chair across from her with the ease of someone who had been receiving visitors all her professional life. "For the newsletter."

"For the regional continuing education bulletin, yes. They've asked for something on practical applications. I thought I'd consult someone who had actually taught Bond technique rather than only audited it."

"You've audited Bond work for how long now? Thirty years?"

"About that."

"Then you probably know as much about practical applications as most teachers." She said it without flattery, as an assessment. "But ask what you like. I enjoy talking about it."

Mira had prepared her questions carefully, in the way she prepared everything: with structure beneath the surface. She began with the genuinely innocuous ones about the history of Bond technique in the provincial curriculum, and Oksana answered with the pleasure of a person discussing a subject she loved, and the conversation had the comfortable rhythm of an interview going well.

After twenty minutes she said: "I've been trying to understand the doubled-signature phenomenon in Bond casting. For the piece. The way the residue layers overlap."

"The phase offset," Oksana said, nodding. "Yes, it's one of the things that confuses students initially. The amplified caster's signature and the amplifying caster's signature don't simply add: they layer, with a slight temporal offset, because the amplifying casting occurs fractionally after the initiated casting. You can read the offset with a Master-tier lens if you know what to look for."

"And if the Bond is cast through ambient residue rather than through an active caster?"

A very brief pause. So brief that someone without thirty years of listening for the pauses in what people said would not have noticed it.

"That's not standard technique," Oksana said. "Theoretically, ambient residue doesn't have the coherence to serve as a carrier. You'd need a live license signature."

"Theoretically," Mira said.

"Yes." Oksana looked at her with the attention of a woman who was deciding what to say. "In practice, there are historical records of experimental techniques that attempted something like that. Pre-Registry. Most were unsuccessful. The residue disperses too quickly."

"Most?"

"There are always outliers in the historical record." She smiled, which was the professional smile of someone managing a conversation. "Were you looking for something specific for the piece?"

"Just thoroughness." Mira made a note on her pad that said nothing useful. "I'm also curious about defensive ward architectures in relation to Bond technique. The way a ward pattern reflects the teacher's methodology."

"Ah." This was a more comfortable topic and Oksana visibly relaxed into it. "Yes, that's one of the things I always tell my students: your defensive architecture is your signature in the most literal sense. It's how you were taught to think about protection. I can tell within a few minutes of watching someone cast a ward whether they trained in the Guild's central facilities or in the provincial circuit. The central curriculum emphasizes perimeter-out construction. Provincial teachers, especially the pre-standardization ones, tended toward compressed-core."

"And your students use your approach?"

"The good ones do," she said, with a warmth that was entirely real. "It's more efficient, actually, though the Guild standardized away from it. A compressed-core ward holds under higher ambient pressure because the force is concentrated rather than distributed. Better for close-quarters situations."

She paused, and in the pause poured herself more tea with the comfortable automaticity of someone doing something they'd done a thousand times in conversation, and looked at the window, which showed the grey mid-morning sky above the garden wall.

"It's a methodology that gets taught differently depending on who's teaching it," she said. "The Guild's standardized approach prioritizes reproducibility. The same ward, cast by any practitioner at the same Tier, produces roughly the same result. That's useful for regulatory purposes. It means an auditor can read a ward and know within a reasonable margin what to expect from it." She smiled slightly. "It also means that every practitioner trained in the last twenty years casts a ward that looks the same as every other practitioner trained in the last twenty years. It flattens the individual characteristics out of the work."
"You prefer the individual characteristics," Mira said.
"I prefer the precision. When you teach from first principles, the student learns why the compression works and what the force dynamics are doing at each point in the structure. They build the ward that the principles require, not the ward that the curriculum permits. The result is that each student's ward is their own. I can look at a ward cast by someone who trained with me fifteen years ago and see my own teaching in it." She looked at her tea. "It's rather like handwriting, in that way. You can identify a person by it even from a considerable distance."
"Even if the person is no longer in contact with you?"
"The methodology persists." She said it simply, as a fact, and then was quiet for a moment in the way of someone who has said something accurate and finds it unexpectedly heavy. "Cornelius's wards were immediately recognizable to me when I encountered them later in his career. He had internalized the compression principle completely. He had, in that respect, very good form."
She said "had" without emphasis. The past tense of a teacher talking about a student who was dead. Mira made a note.

She was talking about the ward Mira had read on Cornelius Veld's desk. She was talking about it from the position of the teacher, which was also, if Mira was right, the position of the person who had seen it cast in the last moments before the casting that killed him.

Mira made another note. She wrote: compressed-core, provincial tradition, pre-standardization. She underlined provincial tradition.

"You taught Cornelius Veld," she said. "When he was young."

"For two years. He was eighteen when he came to me, before his formal Practitioner training." She looked at the window for a moment. The garden sound came through, just audible. "He was one of the people who stayed."

"Stayed?"

"Maintained the relationship. After the formal instruction ends, most students go their own way. A few stay in contact. He was one of those." She was quiet for a moment. "He did use a compressed-core structure. I noticed it in his work, years later, and I told him so, and he was pleased. He liked to know where things came from."

She said this in the specific way of a person who had kept count, without drama, because the count itself said something they had accepted about how the world worked. Most students went their own way. Some stayed. Cornelius had stayed. Mira thought about what that meant: thirty-five years of dinners, garden plants, and conversations about theoretical work. Somewhere in those thirty-five years, something had been said in the ease of an established relationship that had felt safe enough to say, and had not been.

"What did you talk about," Mira said, "when you had dinner. In the recent years."

"History, mostly. He became very interested in pre-Registry technique about three years ago. I think a client had asked him about some historical application he hadn't encountered before, and it opened a door." She set down her cup. "He started reading widely. He had access to some of the older Guild materials through his practitioner registration, and he acquired some texts privately as well. He came to our dinners with questions."

"And you answered them."

"When I could." She said this without weight, as a statement of fact. "Historical technique is my area of expertise. It was natural. He asked and I answered and the conversations were good." A pause. "He had very good questions."

Mira wrote this down and underlined it: *Three years ago. Client inquiry. Reading widely. Private texts.* The annotation on Cornelius's teaching record at the Guild: *professional contact with prior instructor, Year 31.* Three years ago. The same window.

She said this with the genuine grief of someone remembering, and Mira sat with it. The conversation finished its tea and wound itself to a natural close. Mira left with her notebook and her pretext, and she took the long way home.

She was not suspicious yet. She was not ready to be suspicious yet, or rather, she was and she was managing the readiness very carefully. What she had confirmed was not new information so much as the architecture of information she already had: the compressed-core ward, Oksana's teaching, Cornelius's decades in the orbit of a woman who had a theoretical knowledge of experimental Bond technique and had been present at an incident involving an Archived spell.

She went home and wrote it all down precisely. Then she opened her reference materials. Then she looked at a provincial licensing database she had access to through the office. There she found something that was not an absence of information but a presence of it, and it was, she thought, the thing that had been waiting for her to look directly at it.

CHAPTER TWELVE

A Gap in the Records

The provincial licensing database was not, in itself, a difficult thing to access. Any licensed practitioner could view their own records; any registered employer could view the records of practitioners in their employ; any auditor could request records relevant to an active audit. Mira had audit authority on the Veld file, which was still technically open pending the investigation, and she had used this authority to request a records pull on all licensed practitioners with significant commercial activity in the province over the past decade.

She had not, when she submitted this request, been thinking about Oksana Rael specifically. She had been thinking about the supplier chain: who in the province had the professional profile consistent with knowledge of Archived compound components, and how would their licensing history reflect it. She was looking for patterns. She found a pattern she had not been looking for.

Oksana Rael's Master-tier license showed a fourteen-month lapse in renewal, beginning twenty-eight years ago and concluding with a reinstatement that appeared in the records without explanation. The lapse was not unusual in itself: licenses lapsed sometimes due to administrative delay, health issues, financial difficulty, relocation across provincial boundaries. What was unusual was where Oksana had been during the lapse.

The reinstatement application, which she cross-referenced from the Guild's administrative archive, listed a return address in the Haverscroft District. She recognized the name: a cluster of rural parishes on the provincial border, the sort of place that appeared in enforcement briefings and not much else. The regional gazetteer confirmed what she already half-knew: the Haverscroft District was historically characterized by low magical industry, minimal regulatory infrastructure, and what the gazetteer described in its diplomatic way as "a tradition of informal casting practice predating the Registry." In the vocabulary of the licensing community, "informal casting practice predating the Registry" meant exactly one thing: it was a place where unlicensed casting had historically been tolerated, where practitioners without formal Guild registration had operated, and where, consequently, the sort of trade that required keeping away from official records had tended to concentrate.

She had known the Haverscroft District by professional reputation for years. She had never been there herself, but she had colleagues who had: enforcement officers, mostly, doing the periodic sweeps that the Guild conducted in regions with elevated informal casting rates. The sweeps rarely caught anything significant. They were, if she was honest, mostly a way for the Guild to demonstrate that it was paying attention.

Oksana Rael had lived in the Haverscroft District for fourteen months. She had arrived there about three years after the incident at the Guild's Provincial Training Annex, long enough after to confirm that no serious investigation was coming, long enough to establish herself in the place she was going. She had reinstated her license and returned to registered practice fourteen months after that.

Mira sat with the arithmetic for a long time.

About three years after casting the Severing Cascade in the demonstration hall, if she had cast it, Oksana Rael had relocated to a region known for informal casting networks. She had spent fourteen months there. She had then returned, relicensed, and resumed her career with the unbroken professional reputation of a woman who had taken a sabbatical.

She could have gone there to practice. To develop the technique further, in conditions where the residue-monitoring that governed licensed practice did not apply. She could have gone there to make contacts: people who dealt in Archived knowledge, in discontinued formulations, in the kind of underground expertise that could not be transacted through official channels. She could have gone there to establish something she would spend the next twenty-six years building.

Or she could have gone there because she was burnt-out, or because she had a personal crisis, or because she had always wanted to live in the Haverscroft District, and the timing was nothing more than a coincidence of a particularly unfortunate kind.

Mira did not believe in coincidences of this shape. She believed in them as a category, in the way she believed in all categories: as useful approximations of reality that needed to be tested against the specifics. The specific here was that the pattern of Oksana's career break aligned, in timing, location, and professional implication, with every other pattern she had been finding.

She pulled up the provincial registration records for licensed practitioners who had trained under Oksana Rael in the past fifteen years. The Guild maintained teaching-credit records for Master-tier casters who ran recognized instruction programs; it was part of the continuing education framework. Oksana's teaching record covered twenty-three students, most of them practitioners now licensed at Journeyman or Tier 2 level, several of whom had gone on to advanced licensing. The list included a name she recognized.

Cornelius Veld. Licensed under Oksana Rael's instruction credit, year eight of the Registry's current period. Two years of private theory instruction, beginning when Veld was eighteen.

She knew this already from the conversation at the memorial. What she had not known was that the teaching record included contact annotations: brief notes made by the Guild's tracking office when a student's subsequent career intersected with the teaching record in reportable ways. Most of the annotations were routine: license renewals, Tier upgrades, the ordinary administrative life of a practicing caster.

The annotation on Cornelius Veld's entry was not routine. It read: Licensee reported contact with prior instructor re: professional matter, Year 31 of current period. No formal record created.

Year 31. Three years ago. A contact between Veld and Oksana that had been noted as professional in nature but had not generated a formal record. Which meant someone at the Guild had been told about it, informally, and had noted it informally, and had not pursued it.

She did not know what the contact had been about. She could infer a range of things and preferred not to infer without evidence. She wrote down the annotation precisely and drew a line from it to the selenite dust entry in her working notes.

Three years ago: professional contact between Veld and Oksana. Seven weeks ago: Veld wrote to the Archival Division.

Four weeks ago: selenite dust purchased. One week ago: Veld's death.

She had a timeline now. She had a location history. She had a teaching connection. She had a teaching style that matched the ward pattern on the dead man's desk.

She did not have proof of the casting. Everything she had was pattern and inference and the residue reading from Friday morning that she had not shared with Inspector Brenn.

She needed one more thing. She needed the procurement chain: who had known about the selenite dust, who had supplied the knowledge of what it was for, who had provided the technical information that a Tier 3 practitioner in a Cooper Lane enchantment shop would not have had on his own.

She needed to go back to the beginning of the ledger entry and follow it further than she had.

She did not go back to the ledger entry that day.

She went, instead, to the Merchant's Quarter walk-through that was on the schedule, because the schedule was one of the things that had held her in place for thirty years, and because walking through a dozen Tier 1 renewal checks was, at this moment, a form of medicine. She checked the weather-adjustment enchantment on the wool merchant's east wall: Tier 1, clean, two years since last calibration, within acceptable range. The cold-storage spell at the fishmonger's: Tier 1, clean, the same casting she had audited three years ago and found adequately maintained. The decorative light-work on the tea-house facade: Tier 1, clean, slightly warmer than registered but within the variance limit, a note to self to flag at next renewal. She moved through the quarter with Prudence and her notebook and the orderliness of someone whose professional self was functioning correctly while something underneath it was not.

She was very good at this. She had been very good at it for thirty years.

The wool merchant, a man named Hessie whose enchantment had been clean in every audit for the nine years she had been reviewing it, offered her a cup of tea and she took it and stood in his back office for ten minutes talking about the autumn wool prices. She listened and thought, behind her listening face, about Oksana's fourteen-month absence and the specific chain of procurement she had been building for two weeks, and about the fact that what she had was not yet proof and might not become proof through the channels available to her.

The Merchant's Quarter walk took most of the morning. She was done by noon and went directly from the last renewal to a meeting she had arranged the previous afternoon, with the aide to Councilor Vanya Bright, which she had described in her message as a routine inquiry into the commercial contracting record of a recently deceased licensed practitioner.

The Councilor's administrative office occupied the upper floor of the provincial government building on the east side of the square: a well-maintained room with good windows and the specific orderliness of a space that was important enough to be kept presentable but not important enough for anyone to care about its character. The aide, a young man named Treviss who wore the harried efficiency of someone managing two councilors' schedules simultaneously, found her a chair and sat across from her with a folder.

"The Council contracts with Veld's Enchantments are straightforward," he said, with the preemptive tidiness of someone who had already anticipated what an auditor from the Licensing Office would want to know. "Three annual contracts, renewed each year, all through competitive tender. The rates are on the lower end of the tendered range, but not unusually so for a practitioner with that level of experience and a long-standing client relationship."

"Who signed off on the tenders, on the Council side?"

"The Commerce Committee. Standard procedure. The Councilor oversees the committee but doesn't personally review individual contracts below a certain value threshold."

"Has the Councilor had any direct contact with the business? Either of the partners?"

Treviss consulted his folder. "There's a note here that the Councilor attended the opening of the new stockroom last spring. It was a small industry event, a few dozen local businesses. She attended as a representative of the Commerce Committee's small enterprise initiative." He paused. "She was one of perhaps forty people. I don't believe she had a personal relationship with either Mr. Veld or his partner."

Mira noted this and moved on. "Were there any contract amendments in the past year? Any changes to the scope or rate of the existing contracts?"

Treviss looked at his folder more carefully. "There's a proposal in here from about four months ago. An amendment to the acoustics enchantment contract, extending the calibration scope to include some pre-Registry resonance work in the old council chamber. The proposal came from the business side, signed by Petter Haas." He paused. "It was declined. The Commerce Committee voted it down because the pre-Registry scope would require a specialist sign-off outside the standard contracting process."

Pre-Registry resonance work. She wrote this down carefully. A contract amendment proposing work in a pre-Registry technical scope, declined on procedural grounds. Haas had brought this proposal to the Council four months ago, which was approximately concurrent with the period when Oksana had sourced the selenite dust through Petra Vane.

She did not know what to make of this yet. It could be coincidence: a commercial contractor trying to expand his billing scope into specialized territory. It could be a man who had been told that pre-Registry technique was available through channels he had access to, and who had tried to monetize that access through the most straightforward route he could see. It was a pattern piece, sitting beside the other pattern pieces, not yet fitted.

"One more thing," she said. "The Councilor attended Mr. Veld's memorial, I believe? Or sent flowers."

"Both," Treviss said. He checked a different folder. "She attended briefly. It was the day after the arrest on the fraud charges. She went privately, with no staff, which was somewhat unusual. I have a note here that she had asked for the address separately from the announcement."

Mira looked at her notebook. "Thank you," she said. "This has been very helpful."

She walked out of the provincial building and stood for a moment in the cool grey air of the square. The Councilor had attended the memorial privately, the day after Haas's arrest, without staff, having asked for the address separately. This was either the action of a person who had known Cornelius Veld better than the official record suggested, or the action of a person in distress about the arrest of a man she had contracted with for several years, or it was nothing more than a private expression of condolence from a public official who had found her own way to observe something she felt she owed.

It was not evidence of anything. It was something she would sit with.

She walked back to the Licensing Office and told Bram the walk-through had been entirely clean.

"I know," he said, with the faint satisfaction of a man whose district was well-maintained. "I'd have been surprised otherwise."

She sat at her desk and thought about the Councilor attending a memorial privately, and about Haas proposing a pre-Registry contract amendment, and about all the places in a provincial town where knowledge could move through informal channels if someone knew the channels and had operated them carefully for nearly thirty years.

She was one more step away from the name that kept appearing at the end of every line she drew. She needed Oksana Rael's residue baseline, and she needed it before the crime scene signature degraded any further, and she needed a pretext that would not trigger the problem she was not yet ready to trigger.

She took out a piece of Guild notepaper.

CHAPTER THIRTEEN

Delia Knows Something

The estate audit was legitimate. When a licensed practitioner died without a completed succession plan, the Licensing Office had an obligation to assess the outstanding commercial obligations and determine the status of any registered equipment and active enchantments. Delia Veld had agreed to it two days after the memorial, in the efficient, practical tone of someone who had a lot to organize and was organizing it methodically.

They met at the shop on Friday, two weeks after Cornelius Veld's death. Delia had been given access to the premises once the Inspector's initial assessment concluded, and she had spent the intervening time doing, Mira could see, what she had told Brenn she intended to do: figuring out whether the business was viable. The shop was cleaner than it had been at the memorial. Someone had straightened the demonstration stand and restocked the display cases. The ledger was on the counter with a series of colored markers in it.

"I appreciate you coming," Delia said. She was wearing a work coat, which told Mira she had not come straight from somewhere else but had planned to be here, working. "I know this isn't the most straightforward situation."

"It rarely is, in these circumstances," Mira said. "I'll need to review the equipment registrations for transfer or suspension, and the outstanding commission contracts for liability assessment. If you've had a chance to look at those already, it will save us time."

Delia had had a chance to look at them. She had a folder ready. She was, Mira was beginning to understand, a woman with a great deal of practical intelligence that had been largely devoted to not engaging with her father's professional life, and now that she was engaging with it, she was doing so with impressive efficiency.

They worked through the audit materials for an hour. Delia answered questions clearly and without elaboration, which was the correct approach. She had the bookkeeping background that came from doing the accounts for the shop during two periods when her father had been ill. She knew where things were.

She asked good questions. Mira had worked with the families of deceased practitioners before. The succession process was a standard part of the estate audit, and she had done it perhaps twenty times in thirty years. The range of what families brought to these conversations was wide. Delia brought precision and a complete absence of sentimentality about the material, which was both efficient and, Mira found, its own form of evident love: the love that expressed itself by understanding what the deceased had valued and treating it accordingly.

Midway through the commission review, Delia set down the folder she was holding and picked up a second one from the shelf behind her. "This was his reference system," she said. "For the active commissions. He kept the contracts in the main file and his working notes separately." She handed it across.

Mira opened it. Cornelius Veld's working notes had the specific density of a mind that thought by annotating: each commission had a main contract entry and beside it a series of observations in his slightly cramped hand, observations about the casting conditions, the equipment variables, the client's preferences, the challenges of the space. They were thorough past the point of requirement. They were the notes of a man who intended to do each job well and kept records so that well could be reproduced.

"He used a compressed-core approach for the smaller environmental castings," Delia said. She said it with the ease of someone who had grown up around the vocabulary. "He said it was more efficient. His teacher had shown him the technique when he was young."

She said "his teacher" without inflection. She did not say the name. Mira wrote nothing in her notebook.

It was during the review of the outstanding commissions that Mira said, without emphasis: "Your father seemed preoccupied when I was here for the annual audit two weeks ago. Was he under unusual professional pressure?"

Delia looked at the folder in her hands. "You're not only here for the estate audit."

"I'm primarily here for the estate audit," Mira said.

A moment of silence that was, she thought, a decision being made.

"He was frightened," Delia said. "In the last few weeks. He was careful not to show it but I know what my father looked like when he was trying not to show something, and it was different from his ordinary worrying." She paused. "He said something to me about three weeks before he died. We were having dinner, which we did most Sundays, and he said, there is something wrong with my understanding of a situation, and I am trying to determine whether I have been misled or whether I have been unfair." She looked up. "That's almost exactly what he said. He was very precise in his language."

"Did he say which situation?"

"Not at first." She set the folder down and straightened it. "I asked. He said it involved someone he trusted and that he hoped he was wrong. He said he had been going back through some materials and had found something he couldn't account for." She paused again. "I asked if I could help. He said no, it was historical, it required access to records he was trying to get."

She had said all of this in the measured tone of someone reporting facts. Now her expression shifted, slightly, toward something more complex.

"I didn't ask more. I thought, if he wanted help, he would ask for it. He wasn't the sort of person who concealed things because he wanted to burden himself. He concealed things because he had decided he needed to sort them out himself first." She looked at the wall behind Mira's head for a moment. "I should have asked more."

"You couldn't have known," Mira said.

"I chose not to know." Delia said it flatly, without seeking absolution. "There's a difference." She looked at Mira directly. "I think you understand the difference."

This was said with the precision of someone who had been thinking about it. Mira, who did understand the difference, said nothing.

"He mentioned Oksana Rael," Delia said. "That's what I wanted to tell you. I wasn't going to, because I don't know what it means, but you asked about the situation and I think it's what he was talking about. He said something wrong with the situation, and then he said her name, and then he stopped talking about it." She looked at the folder again. "He had known her since he was young. She was important to him. I think whatever he found was very difficult."

Mira wrote Oksana Rael's name in her notebook, which was unnecessary since it was already there in several places, but sometimes writing a name was not about adding information.

"One more thing," Delia said. She opened the folder to a tabbed section Mira had not been shown yet. "When I was doing the accounts during his illness, two years ago, I found an invoice in the supplier file that was different from the others. It was from Aldwick Specialty Ingredients, which was a regular supplier, but it had a note on it I didn't understand. It said, per consultation, with an initial I didn't recognize." She handed Mira the invoice copy. "The initial is R.O. The consultation charge was separate from the ingredient charge. It was modest. I didn't ask about it at the time."

Mira looked at the invoice. Per consultation, ref: R.O. The consultation charge was fifteen ducats, which was modest indeed for any professional consultation. The ingredient on the invoice was not selenite dust but something called calibrated quartz suspension, which was also a pre-Registry compound component, also with limited current application.

"R.O.," she said.

"Yes," Delia said.

Mira took a copy of the invoice. She finished the estate audit in a professional and thorough manner. She issued the preliminary assessment of the outstanding commissions and the recommended status for the registered equipment and told Delia she would have the full report within five working days.

She walked back to the Licensing Office in the kind of focused silence that she used when she was not yet ready to think about something directly and was letting it arrange itself in the background. She had Oksana Rael's initials on an invoice from two years ago. She had a consultation charge. She had a meeting between a retired Master-tier caster and a specialty ingredient supplier, documented in a paper trail that the retired Master-tier caster could not have known existed.

She had the supplier's address in the folder she always carried. She had tomorrow free.

CHAPTER FOURTEEN

The Supplier

Aldwick Specialty Ingredients occupied a narrow building on a narrow street in the commercial quarter's eastern annex, which was not a part of Thornhallow that attracted much foot traffic or much official attention. The sign above the door was small and factual: the business name, the license number, the hours. No decorative claims, no display of samples. The sort of establishment that preferred to be found by people who already knew it was there.

Nestor Aldwick was perhaps fifty-five, with the general appearance of a man who spent most of his time managing paperwork in a small room and was comfortable with this. He looked at Mira's auditor's credentials with the resigned recognition of someone who had been audited before and had always passed.

"Miss Ashcroft. The Thornhallow office." He gestured to a chair in front of the counter. "What can I help you with?"

"I'm following up on a commercial transaction recorded in the audit file of a recently deceased client. Cornelius Veld, Veld's Enchantments, Cooper Lane."

"I heard about Mr. Veld. Sad business." He pulled up the records without being asked: a man who knew the correct procedure. "The Veld account. Yes. A recent transaction, about a month ago. Twenty grams of preserved selenite dust."

"Can you tell me what preceded the transaction? Whether there was any inquiry or consultation before the purchase was made?"

He looked at the record. "He came in to discuss the compound about a week before he placed the order. Standard practice for unusual purchases. I try to make sure clients understand what they're purchasing."

"What did he say he wanted it for?"

"He said he was researching historical compound work. The selenite dust has some obscure historical applications. He wanted to understand the provenance and properties." A pause. "He was a careful man. He asked good questions."

"Did he indicate where his interest in the compound originated? Whether someone had recommended it to him?"

Aldwick was quiet for a moment, in the way of a man who was deciding whether a question crossed a line he was comfortable with.

"He mentioned that he'd been discussing some pre-Registry formulations with a former teacher," he said finally. "He didn't name anyone. He said the teacher had mentioned selenite dust in the context of some historical work they'd been discussing."

Mira made a careful note. "I want to ask about another transaction. An earlier one, from approximately two years ago. An invoice in the Veld account references a consultation charge, initial R.O."

"That would be a third-party consultation," Aldwick said. He pulled up a different record. "Sometimes a client comes in on the recommendation of a specialist, and the specialist has an arrangement with us for a referral acknowledgment. Standard in the specialty trade."

"And who was R.O.?"

He looked at the record for a moment. Then he looked at Mira with the careful expression of a man who was going to tell the truth and knew it might matter.

"The referral was from Oksana Rael," he said. "She's sent several clients our way over the years. Retired Master-tier caster, lives on Rael Street. She has a considerable knowledge of pre-Registry formulations and she refers clients to us when they need unusual components."

"Does she ever purchase from you herself?"

"Occasionally. The last purchase directly on her account was some time ago." He checked the record. "Four years. Nothing since."

"And through intermediaries?"

A longer pause. He was a careful man, Mira thought, in the way that people were careful when they operated in a space that was technically legal and wanted to stay that way.

"About six months ago," he said slowly, "I had a client come in with a specific list of components. One of them was preserved selenite dust, a similar quantity to what Mr. Veld purchased. The client said they were purchasing on behalf of a research consultation." He paused again. "The client was a young woman. She gave Rael Street as the billing address for the order."

"Did you take a name?"

"I did. I always do, for unusual components." He read from the record. "Petra Vane. She gave the East District practitioner training center as her own address."

Mira wrote the name down. Petra Vane. She knew the name from somewhere. She turned it over in her memory and found it: the teaching records. Oksana's list of former students. Petra Vane had received private theory instruction from Oksana four years ago, now worked as a theory instructor at the East District training center. Young, perhaps twenty-five. A former student. A current professional contact.

"Did Ms. Vane give any indication of what the components were for?" she asked.

"She said they were for a research project. She didn't elaborate." He paused once more. "She seemed," he said carefully, "unaware of the specific applications of what she was purchasing. She had a list. She purchased what was on the list. I don't believe she had any particular knowledge of the compound's history."

An unknowing intermediary. A young woman given a shopping list, told it was for a research project, with no reason to question the instruction from a teacher she presumably trusted and respected.

Mira thought about that for a moment. She thought about what it said about the person who had designed this arrangement: meticulous, cautious, and entirely willing to use a young woman's trust as a tool.

She thanked Nestor Aldwick, who watched her go with the expression of a man who had told a truth and was not sure what it would cost him.

She stood on the narrow street for a moment in the early autumn light and thought about what she had.

She had a chain: Oksana to Petra Vane to the ingredient purchase to Cornelius Veld. She had the mechanism: the teaching relationship that gave Oksana access to an unknowing buyer, and the referral relationship that gave her access to the supplier without appearing in the purchase records herself. She had the timeline: six months before Veld's death, Oksana had acquired the materials through Petra Vane. She had then, Mira inferred, given the selenite dust to Veld as part of the historical discussion that had led him toward the research he couldn't quite complete before he realized what he was researching.

Or she had kept it for herself. She had never given it to Veld at all. The selenite dust in Veld's ledger might have come to him through an entirely different channel, and the Aldwick purchase six months ago might have been the practice run: Oksana acquiring the component to use in the casting, not to pass on.

She needed to read Oksana's residue. She needed to read it directly, against a baseline, with Prudence in a good light, and she needed Oksana's license number in her lens while she did it.

She needed to find a pretext for that which was better than the Bond technique newsletter piece.

She went home and thought about pretexts.

CHAPTER FIFTEEN

Brenn Makes an Arrest

She was at the office early the next morning, which was unusual. Bram arrived at the normal hour and looked at her with the expression that had been appearing with more frequency recently: the one where he was clearly aware something was wrong and was deciding how to approach it. He decided, as he sometimes did, by putting the kettle on and then sitting across from her desk. He spoke with the directness that was his form of care: "You've been coming in early, staying late, and you're not reviewing the standard files. I'm not asking about the investigation. I'm asking if you're all right."

"I'm working through something," she said.

"I know. I can see you working through something." He paused, selecting his words. "You've had a look. For about two weeks now. The specific one where you're here and also somewhere else and the somewhere else is not a good place."

"That's a specific description."

"I've been your colleague for seven years," he said. "I've learned the vocabulary."

She looked at the folder in front of her, which was the Aldwick correspondence she had gone over three times the previous evening. She had the feeling she sometimes had late in complex audits: that all the pieces were present and she was moving them in slightly the wrong configuration. That the pattern was about to reveal itself and she was one turn short of seeing it.

"I'll tell you," she said. "When I've resolved it. I'll tell you the whole thing."

He nodded. He refilled her tea from the kettle and stood up. At the doorframe he stopped. "The grey archival box," he said. It was neither a question nor a statement. She had mentioned it once, three years ago, in a conversation about professional records management, and had not mentioned it again.

"Yes," she said.

He looked at her for one moment. "Then I'll wait," he said, and went back to his desk.

He called her on a Monday morning. He called her on her official contact number, which was the Licensing Office line, and Bram answered and put it through to her with the face of a man who was trying not to be visibly curious.

"I wanted to let you know," Brenn said, "as a professional courtesy, before you saw it in the provincial bulletin. We've made an arrest."

She had known, when she heard the steadiness of his opening sentence, what the arrest was.

"Petter Haas," she said.

"Yes." A pause. "The alibi information you provided was central. The supplier statement confirmed the timeline gap. Combined with the commission fraud and the evidence of a deteriorating partnership, we have a solid case for criminal investigation into the licensing violations and the question of opportunity. The licensing fraud alone is a serious offense. A Tier 3 practitioner billing Tier 4 rates on commercial contracts is a category-two misrepresentation."

"I know what it is," she said.

"I know you do." Another pause. "The murder determination is still provisional. The Guild's regional forensic team has confirmed accidental self-cast as the working conclusion. The arrest is on the fraud charges, with the investigation into his activities on the morning of the death continuing as a separate matter."

She held this in her mind. An arrest on the fraud charges. A continuing investigation. The official cause of death still accidental.

"Inspector Brenn," she said. "May I come to see you this afternoon?"

She was at his office at two o'clock. He had the kind of office that provincial inspectors had: a desk with too much paper on it, a window onto a courtyard, a filing system that was clearly his own invention and appeared to be working. He offered her tea, which she accepted, and they sat on either side of the desk in the way people sat when they were going to say something difficult.

"I should have told you this sooner," she said. "I'm aware of that."

"Tell me now."

She told him what she had read in the shop on Friday morning. The doubled signature. The Bond overlay. The shape of the casting that had led her to the Severing Cascade. She told him precisely and in the correct order, and she put her notebook on his desk so he could see the notation she had made at the time:

Doubled residue signature. Bond technique. Spell, archived, identity unclear. Secondary license incomplete. Cannot rule out deliberate masking.

Brenn read it. He read it twice. His face went through several things that she recognized, from a professional distance, as the face of a very good Journeyman auditor encountering something that was beyond his reading range and understanding it for the first time.

"You saw this," he said slowly, "on the morning you found him."

"Yes."

"And you didn't tell me."

"No."

He sat with this for a moment with the stillness of someone deciding whether to be angry and concluding that anger was not, right now, the priority.

"Walk me through what this means," he said. "For the investigation."

She walked him through it: the Archived spell, the Bond technique that had masked the second caster's signature, the fact that this ruled out self-cast overstep as a cause because the Severing Cascade required an external caster. She explained what a doubled signature meant. She explained why his lens had not shown him what Prudence had shown her.

When she finished he was quiet for a long time.

"You're the only one who saw this," he said at last.

"Yes."

"The Guild's forensic team confirmed accidental. Their lens reading was at Journeyman level."

"Yes."

"If I'm going to overturn a Guild forensic determination on the basis of a single auditor's reading, that auditor needs to be willing to put it on record. Formally. In a statement that can be challenged."

"I know."

"And Haas," he said. "If this is right, and the death was a deliberate casting by an external party with knowledge of an Archived spell, then Haas didn't kill him."

"He's still guilty of the fraud."

"Yes. But the fraud is not a capital matter." He looked at her steadily. "Miss Ashcroft. I need to understand why you didn't tell me this when you found him."

She had prepared herself for this question. She had prepared an answer that was truthful and incomplete, the same category of answer she had been giving since the morning she stood in the shop and let Brenn build his self-cast theory in peace. She looked at it now, and found that she was tired of it.

"Because," she said, "following the residue reading to its logical conclusion requires opening a sealed Guild incident report from thirty years ago, and my name is on that report in a way that is professionally and personally uncomfortable."

Brenn looked at her. He said nothing for a long moment.

"What's the report number?" he said finally.

"IR-34-071."

He wrote it down. His expression was the careful, neutral expression of a man who had encountered something he did not yet fully understand but was going to.

"I'll need a formal statement from you on the residue reading," he said. "As detailed as possible. And I'll need to understand your connection to IR-34-071 before I can proceed."

"I'll write the statement tonight," she said.

She walked home from the Inspector's office in the early evening, which was darker now than it had been when she first walked this route, autumn settled firmly into itself. She thought about what she had just done, which was less than she needed to do and more than she had been able to bring herself to do for the past two and a half weeks.

She had put Haas's innocence on record. She had complicated the official finding. She had not yet named a suspect or provided the full chain of evidence, but she had created a situation in which the investigation had to continue, which was different from where it had been this morning.

She went home and wrote the statement. She wrote it accurately, which meant she wrote "the Severing Cascade" and she wrote "Bond technique" and she wrote "secondary license signature, unidentified, deliberately masked." She wrote it in the careful language of a professional who was putting something on record that she knew would have consequences.

She did not sleep.

CHAPTER SIXTEEN

The Letter, Read Properly

She had read Cornelius Veld's letter three times since taking it from Tam Finch. She knew it well enough to recite it. She had read it in the park the afternoon she found it, and she had read it at the kitchen table that night with the incident report beside it, and she had read it a third time when she was trying to understand the timeline and needed the dates in front of her.

On the fourth reading she found what she had missed.

It was a Tuesday evening, eighteen days after Veld's death, and she was at the kitchen table with the letter and her working notes and a cup of tea that had gone cold. She was not looking for anything in particular. She was re-reading in the way that she sometimes did, late in an investigation, letting the documents sit differently in her attention now that she knew more than she had when she first read them. The process was not strategic. It was a professional habit that had occasionally produced something valuable.

She found it in the third paragraph, which she had read before as a straightforward account of how Veld had come to suspect the official incident report was inaccurate. The paragraph read:

The information I have received concerns the casting responsible for the incident. I had occasion recently to hear a description of the event from someone who was present, and certain details they provided are inconsistent with the attributed cause in ways that seem significant.

She had read this as: a person who was present described the incident to Veld in a way that raised doubts. She had been looking for what the description contained, what specific detail had been inconsistent. She had not found anything in the letter that answered this question, because the letter did not specify: Veld had been discreet, noting the inconsistency without naming it.

She read the paragraph again. And then she read the paragraph before it:

My grounds for requesting access are as follows: I have recently come into possession of information suggesting that the cause attributed in this report may be inaccurate. I am not a legal professional and cannot assess the implications of this, but I believe the Guild should be made aware of this possibility.

And then she read what she had not read carefully before: the phrase at the beginning of the third paragraph. Not "I had occasion to hear about the incident" but "I had occasion to hear a description of the event from someone who was present."

Cornelius Veld had heard a first-hand description.

He had heard someone who had been in the room describe what had happened. And the description had contained details inconsistent with the attributed cause.

The inconsistency, she now understood, was not what the description said about the accident. It was something the speaker had said about the casting itself. Something in the description that revealed not an alternative account of what had gone wrong, but an account that treated the event as something that had gone right.

She sat with this for a moment and then she went to her working notes where she had written, from the conversation at Oksana's house, the phrase she had found interesting:

He always wanted to understand the theory behind what he was doing.

Oksana had said this at the memorial as well, almost word for word: he wanted to know why. And she had said it at the house: He wanted to understand the theory behind what he was doing.

And then she thought about what Oksana might have said to Cornelius Veld, her devoted former student, in an unguarded dinner conversation or a quiet afternoon discussion. She had been describing some historical casting work, pre-Registry, the kind of theoretical discussion she said she enjoyed having with people who were interested enough to follow. She had described the Severing Cascade, perhaps, as a theoretical example: this was a technique that existed, here is how it worked, here is the principle behind it. She was teaching, which was what she did. And in the course of the teaching she had described the incident at the Provincial Training Annex, perhaps as a documented historical case of a high-tier casting in a controlled setting, and she had said something that revealed, to a careful listener, that she had not been watching an accident but observing her own result.

She had said it worked. Or she had described the cascade effect in the language of someone who had been watching for what they expected rather than reacting to what they feared. Or she had named the pattern as compressed-core architecture and described it correctly before the incident report had been publicly circulated and the pattern could have been known to anyone who hadn't read it with a Master-tier lens.

Or she had simply said: it was a teaching exercise that went right.

Mira did not know what the exact phrase had been. But Cornelius Veld, who was careful, precise, and wanted to understand the theory behind things, had heard it and known something was wrong. He had sat with that knowledge for a while. He had bought selenite dust as a way of understanding what exactly he had heard, and he had written a letter to the Archival Division.

And Oksana Rael had realized, at some point after the dinner conversation or the afternoon discussion, that she had said something she should not have, and that the person she had said it to was the kind of person who would look into it.

Mira now understood the motive completely. She had been treating it as a partial question, knowing that Veld had been about to report something but not knowing exactly what that something was. Now she knew: he had been about to report that Oksana Rael had described the incident in a way that was consistent only with having cast the spell herself. And his letter to the Archival Division, if it had prompted an investigation, would have led a senior auditor to IR-34-071, and a senior auditor reading IR-34-071 with a Master-tier lens would have seen what Mira had seen at twenty-four and had filed as "slightly atypical."

The letter would have led there. Straight to the incident report. Straight to her appended assessment. Straight to the thirty-year-old decision she had made with her supervisor's hand on her shoulder.

So the murder had been not only about protecting Oksana from exposure for the nearly thirty-year knowledge trade she had been running. It had also, secondarily, been about preventing the incident report from being reopened.

She closed the letter and put it very carefully in the middle of the desk.

She thought about what it meant that Oksana had known, in choosing to kill Cornelius Veld, that the path of exposure ran through Mira Ashcroft's own past. She thought about whether Oksana had considered this a coincidental protection or a calculated one.

She thought about this for a long time and did not find a comfortable answer.

CHAPTER SEVENTEEN

What She Could Do

Wednesday was quiet. She worked the morning shift at the Licensing Office, which was her Thursday schedule moved by one day due to a scheduling conflict Bram had with the merchant district walk-through. She reviewed three renewal applications and countersigned two transfers and answered a query from a journeyman practitioner in the west quarter about the documentation required for a Tier upgrade application. The day was correct and ordinary, and she was grateful for it in the way that she was grateful for correct and ordinary things when the alternative was sitting alone in her house with the contents of her working file.

She went home at four and the alternative was waiting.

She had the full picture now. She had the motive, the method, the means, the procurement chain, and the timeline. She had the residue reading from the morning she found the body, notated precisely in a professional notebook that was now part of a formal statement submitted to Inspector Brenn. She had the letter and the incident report and the ghost of a connection that had been sitting in a grey archival box for thirty years.

What she did not have was direct proof that Oksana Rael had cast the Severing Cascade. The doubled signature she had read was proof that the Bond technique had been used and that a second caster was responsible. The second license number was partial and unidentified. The chain of circumstantial evidence was compelling: the teaching, the timeline, the lapse in licensing, the ingredient procurement, the conversation detail Cornelius had recorded in his letter. But circumstantial was not the same as identifying.

To identify Oksana, she needed to read her residue against the signature from the crime scene. She needed the baseline of Oksana's license number in Prudence's lens, compared directly to the partial second signature in her working notes. She needed to be in the same room as Oksana with a legitimate reason to conduct a lens reading.

She could take this to Brenn. She could give him everything she had, let him apply for a formal residue verification order from the Guild's enforcement office, which would allow a licensed official to compel a licensed caster to submit to a residue reading. This was the correct procedure. This was what an Inspector was for.

The procedure would take, at minimum, three weeks. The enforcement office was in the capital. The application required Guild legal review. The timeline for a formal residue verification was established in the regulatory code and was not short.

In three weeks, the partial signature at the crime scene would have degraded to the point where comparison became significantly more difficult. She had perhaps another week of clear reading left, and then another two weeks of partial reading, and after that the distinctive features of the Bond overlay would blur into the ambient residue background. The window was closing.

She could also, she thought, do something else.

The provisional cat arrived on her lap and settled there with the decisive authority of an animal that had decided this was happening regardless of her cooperation. She put her hand on its back in the absent way she had developed, which the cat seemed to find adequate.

Her communication card rang. She looked at the number: her son's prefix in the capital.

"Lev," she said.

"Hello." His voice had his father's pitch, which had always been a mild surprise in her ear even after thirty years. "I tried yesterday and you didn't answer."

"I was working late. I'm sorry."

"I'm not complaining," he said, which was the Lev way of saying that he was slightly concerned and was approaching it from the side. "I just wanted to see how you were. The papers mentioned a death on Cooper Lane. Something to do with a licensed enchantment shop."

"I was the auditor on the account," she said. "I'm involved in the follow-up."

"Are you all right?"

She looked at the window. The autumn light was doing something orange and prolonged outside. "I'm fine. Working through some things."

"Will you come for the winter holiday? We're doing it properly this year. Sanna's family is coming."

She had been meaning to confirm this for three weeks. "I'll try," she said. "I have some things to resolve first."

"You always have some things to resolve," he said, not unkindly. "You know you're allowed to just come without resolving everything first."

"I know," she said, and they both understood this was politely untrue.

They talked for fifteen minutes about Lev's work in the city planning office, about Sanna's family, about the building works near their apartment that had been ongoing for two years with no apparent intention of concluding. These were comfortable topics and she was grateful for them in the way she was grateful for ordinary things. She could hear in his voice that he was monitoring her for something he had not quite identified. She was careful to sound like herself, which was not difficult because she was herself; she was simply herself in the middle of something she had not resolved.

When she ended the call she sat for a while in the orange light with the provisional cat and thought about what she was protecting and what she was afraid of and whether these were the same thing.

She could go to Brenn. She could give him the full chain and the formal statement and let the process unfold over three weeks and accept that the residue comparison might be inconclusive by the time the enforcement office got involved. She could protect the procedure and accept the outcome.

She could go to Oksana herself. She could create a pretext thin enough to hold for the duration of a residue reading and get the baseline she needed and then take it to Brenn with a comparative analysis that would be hard to dismiss. She could move the timeline up by three weeks. She could keep the window open.

She could also do what she had done thirty years ago. She could file the formal statement she had already submitted, let the accidental determination stand for lack of comparative proof, accept that Haas would likely be charged with the fraud and that would be the end of the case, and move on with her audit files, her Tier renewals, and her standing Thursday lunches.

She thought about Cornelius Veld lying carefully on the floor of his clean, well-organized shop. She thought about Harlen Voss, twenty years old, who had spent four weeks in the Guild's medical facility and had never received his Practitioner's license.

She thought about IR-34-071, the thirty-year-old decision, and the fact that she was standing, again, at the exact same junction, with the exact same choice. The only thing that had changed was that she was fifty-four now instead of twenty-four, and she had rather more practice at knowing the difference between what was difficult and what was wrong.

There was a knock at the door, which was Bram's knock: three quick taps, evenly spaced.

She opened it. He was standing on her step with a container of soup in one hand and an apologetic expression.

"I wasn't sure if you'd eaten," he said. "You had the look today."

"What look?"

"The one where you're somewhere else and also here. It's a very specific look. You've had it all week."

She let him in and found bowls and they ate soup at the kitchen table and he did not ask her what was wrong, which was, she thought, one of the more substantial things a person could do for you: not ask the question you could not yet answer. He talked about the merchant district walk-through and a licensing irregularity with a textile enchantment business that was taking up most of his current attention, and she listened and was, genuinely, comforted.

When he left she stood at the kitchen table for a long time.

Then she took out a piece of Guild notepaper and wrote a message to Oksana Rael, requesting a follow-up meeting at her earliest convenience, noting that she was conducting spot verification of provincial Master-tier casters as part of the Guild's continuing education compliance review and that she had some additional questions about Bond technique that she had not had time to address at their first meeting. She noted that the spot verification included a brief residue baseline reading, which was standard procedure for the compliance review, and could be completed in under five minutes.

She posted it that evening.

She did not, as she was walking back from the post box, tell herself that this was the correct procedure. She knew it was not exactly the correct procedure. It was the procedure she was choosing, and the distinction mattered to her, and she preferred to be honest about it.

CHAPTER EIGHTEEN

The Amplification Bond

Oksana Rael replied the next morning. The response was brief and entirely cooperative: she was available on Friday at eleven, she looked forward to seeing Mira again, she had been reading more on the Bond technique subject since their first conversation and had some thoughts she would enjoy sharing. The tone was warm. The warmth had no tremor in it.

Mira read the message and thought about a woman who had been running an underground knowledge trade for nearly thirty years, who had killed a former student she had known for nearly four decades, and who was responding to a follow-up auditing visit with the equanimity of someone who had been doing this sort of thing for a very long time. She was not rattled. She had every reason to believe her technique had been undetectable. The Guild forensic team had confirmed accidental. The Inspector had made an arrest. From where Oksana sat, the situation had resolved.

Mira arrived at Rael Street at eleven on a Friday, which was three weeks after finding Cornelius Veld on his shop floor. She had Prudence in her coat pocket, calibrated that morning, and her official Guild auditor's credentials, and the pretext she had constructed in her letter. She had a professional notebook. She had the partial second signature from her working notes, which she had committed to memory with the precision of someone who had been reading residue for thirty years.

Oksana greeted her at the door as before. Same grey coat. Same posture. Same tea.

"I appreciate your flexibility," Mira said, settling into the chair. "The compliance review is somewhat time-sensitive; the Guild wanted it completed by end of season."

"Of course." Oksana had her own tea poured already. "You mentioned a residue baseline reading. I'll confess it's been many years since anyone asked to take mine. One does forget, in retirement, that the licensing requirements continue."

"It's entirely routine," Mira said. She took out Prudence. "It's simply a record of your license signature as it reads at the current date. For comparison against the registered baseline in your original certification. It helps us verify that the license integrity is maintained." She paused. "May I?"

"Please," Oksana said, and extended her hand across the table in the gesture that Master-tier casters used when consenting to a lens reading: the inner wrist upward, the residue pathways accessible, the posture of professional cooperation.

Mira raised Prudence and looked.

The baseline came up immediately: Oksana Rael's license signature was distinctive in the way that all Master-tier signatures were distinctive, having been built over decades of active casting into something dense and layered and entirely specific. Mira read through the surface layers first, noting the structure, cataloguing the characteristics. It was a genuinely impressive signature: the work of a lifetime of serious casting, complex and well-organized, the magical equivalent of the handwriting of someone who had written beautifully for decades.

She went deeper. Master-tier reading required attention in a way that Journeyman-level work didn't: the lower layers of a caster's signature contained the traces of older work, historical castings that had left their sediment, the ghost residue of things cast years or decades ago that had not fully dissipated. Most people's deeper layers were unremarkable: the ordinary accumulation of a working caster's career, too faded and mixed to be legible as individual events.

She found it in the third layer down.

It was faint, as she had expected. A historical trace, months old at minimum, the kind of residue that formed when a technique had been practiced repeatedly in the same space. Not a single casting but the palimpsest of multiple castings of the same type: the way a musician's fingers bore the calluses of repeated practice. It was a Bond signature. A specific Bond signature. An Amplification Bond cast, not in the legitimate direction, but in the inverted orientation: not amplifying from below but projecting from above, folding a higher-tier casting through a lower-tier carrier.

She read it very carefully. She read it the way she read things that mattered: with Prudence held very still and her breath completely steady and her attention on the pattern rather than on what the pattern was going to mean in the next few minutes.

The compressed-core structure was there. The specific offset timing of the doubled-signature practice runs was there. And beneath it, fainter than the Bond practice signature but present in the way that things present themselves when you know exactly what you're looking for, were traces that matched the partial second signature in her working notes with the specificity of a key fitting a lock.

She had read her comparison notes so many times that she did not need to refer to them. She held the comparison in her memory and she held what Prudence was showing her and she aligned them, and they aligned.

She lowered Prudence.

Oksana was looking at her across the table. They were both very still. The garden sounds came through the window: the same alive-sound as before, a world going about its ordinary business.

"The baseline is consistent with the certification record," Mira said. She wrote something in her notebook: the date, the reference number, and a line of professional notation.

Oksana said nothing. She was watching Mira with the attention of someone who was making a calculation.

"You also mentioned additional questions about Bond technique," she said at last. "From your reading research."

"Yes." Mira capped her pen. "I wanted to ask about the inverted Bond application. The technique in which a higher-tier casting is projected through a lower-tier carrier signature. You described it as historically documented but theoretically unlikely to succeed. I was wondering if there were any practical records of its successful use."

A very long pause.

Oksana's face did not change in any way that would have been visible to someone not watching for it. What Mira saw, over thirty years of reading the pauses in what people said and did not say, was a person completing a calculation and arriving at its conclusion.

"You're not here about the newsletter," Oksana said.

"No," Mira said.

"Or the compliance review."

"No."

Another pause. The garden sounds continued. The tea was still hot.

"And the technique you've just described," Oksana said, "with the inverted Bond and the lower-tier carrier. You found this in my baseline."

"I found traces consistent with repeated practice of this technique, yes."

"And you have a signature from another location that you believe matches these traces."

"Yes."

Oksana looked at her tea. She looked at it for a long time with the expression of someone who had been carrying a very precise and calculated arrangement for a long time and was now watching it come loose at one corner.

"How clear?" she said finally. "The match."

"Clear enough to be significant," Mira said. "Not beyond any possible dispute. But significant."

"And you know about the Archived spell."

"I identified it on the morning of Mr. Veld's death."

Oksana nodded slowly, and for the first time since Mira had walked in she looked her age: not frailer, not less composed, but simply a person who had arrived at the end of a very long calculation. She looked at Mira across the kitchen table with the considering expression of a woman who was deciding how to spend the time she had left.

"I think," she said, "that you had better stay for a little while."

Mira stayed.

CHAPTER NINETEEN

Oksana Speaks

She did not begin with an apology. Mira had not expected her to.

She began, instead, with the Archival system.

"There are four hundred and sixty-two Archived spells in the current Registry," she said. "I've read all the archival documentation. I've read the reasons given for the Archival decisions. Some of them are reasonable. Some of them are political. Some of them are simply old: the Guild archived them because it had decided to standardize, and the standardization was not always the right choice. The Severing Cascade was Archived because of the incident thirty years ago. But the incident thirty years ago was my doing, and the decision to Archive the spell on the basis of my behavior rather than the spell's properties was a category error."

She said this without heat. It was a position she had clearly held for a long time and had refined into something like a formal argument.

"The spell itself," she continued, "is no more dangerous than a dozen other Tier 4 formulations that remained in the Registry. Its properties are specific and controllable. It was Archived because of bad optics, not because of inherent danger. The Guild made a bureaucratic decision and called it a safety decision and the difference between those two things is, in my view, significant."

"You were teaching it," Mira said.

"I was selling knowledge of it. And of other Archived spells, and of discontinued pre-Registry formulations, and of techniques that the Guild had simply decided not to standardize. There is a market for this knowledge. There have always been practitioners who want access to the full range of what is possible, not just the range that has been approved by a licensing board for administrative convenience." She looked at Mira steadily. "I provided this access. For nearly thirty years. I did it carefully and I did it selectively and I did not teach it to people who were going to use it irresponsibly."

She said this without defiance. It was the description of a project, stated plainly.

"How many people?" Mira asked.

"Over thirty years? Directly, perhaps forty. Indirectly, through students of students, more than that, though I don't track the secondary distribution. I don't operate a school. I operate a conversation." She looked at the window. "Most of what I've shared is entirely innocuous by any reasonable standard. Discontinued weather-modification techniques. Pre-Registry compounding methods that the Guild standardized away from because standardization was administratively simpler, not because the techniques were dangerous. The knowledge exists. The Guild chooses not to maintain it in the official record. I maintain it elsewhere."

"And the dangerous techniques?"

"There are a handful. I have been selective about those." She looked at Mira directly. "The Severing Cascade is the most significant. I have not taught it to anyone. What I did with it myself is a separate matter."

"What you used it for yourself."

"Yes." A pause. "And what I used it for, thirty years ago, was different from last month. Thirty years ago I was testing the technique. I needed a real application, real ambient conditions, a real setting to understand what it did in practice. It was a research casting." She said this without flinching. "Harlen Voss was not the target. There was no target. I was determining what the spell's distribution would look like in an uncontrolled ambient setting."

Mira sat with this for a moment. A research casting. A spell used on a room full of people to see what it would do. The description did not make it more acceptable. It made it a different shape of unacceptable.

"He spent four weeks in the medical facility," she said. "He never practiced."

"I know." It was said without defense. "I have thought about Harlen Voss a great many times over the past thirty years. The fact that he was not the intended subject does not resolve anything about what he experienced."

"You used it on Cornelius Veld."

"Yes."

"He was your student."

"Yes." A pause. "He was also the person who was about to report me to the Guild's Archival Division, which would have led to a formal investigation into my activities, which would have resulted in the end of my freedom and likely my license. I was aware of this."

"He was going to report you because of something you told him."

"I was careless," she said. "I have been talking about historical technique for nearly thirty years. I am very good at describing it in ways that maintain plausible distance. I slipped, with Cornelius, because I trusted him. Because I had known him since he was eighteen and I had let my guard down in a way I don't with clients. I described the incident at the training annex in a way that revealed I had been watching what I expected, not reacting to what surprised me." She paused. "He caught it. He was always very precise."

"He was," Mira said.

"I realized afterward. A week later I knew he was looking into it. He cancelled our dinner without explanation, and then I found out from another contact that he had been asking questions about pre-Registry compound components, and I understood what was happening." Her voice was even throughout. "I had time to consider what to do. I considered it for three weeks. I decided that the alternative to acting was unacceptable."

"He trusted you," Mira said.

"He did." She looked up. "I don't offer this as a justification. It's a fact that I find genuinely difficult. He was not a strategic choice. He was someone I cared about." She paused again. "These two things are both true. I don't know what to do with that except acknowledge it."

Mira sat with this for a moment.

She had expected, coming here, that the confirmation of what she already knew would feel like a conclusion. Instead it felt like the beginning of a different kind of problem, with a different kind of weight. Oksana Rael was sitting across from her describing the decision to kill a former student with the same measured, first-principles clarity with which she described the theory of Bond technique: here is the structure of the thing, here is why it works, here is the cost it carries. It was not coldness. It was precision, and Mira recognized it because she possessed something of the same quality herself, and had occasionally wondered what it would look like if it were deployed in the wrong direction.

"He was a better person than most," Oksana said. Not an apology. A statement, with the grief still present in it that had been present at the memorial six weeks ago. "He came to me at eighteen wanting to understand what he was working with. He stayed in my life for thirty-five years wanting to understand what he was working with. He had the patience that real understanding requires, and he had the honesty that comes when you respect the work enough to look at it accurately." She looked at the window. "He looked at me accurately. In the end."

"You recognized it when he did."

"Immediately. He had a specific quality of question when he understood something and was waiting to see if you'd confirm it rather than asking you to contradict it. He asked me about the incident in that way. Not what happened but what you intended." A pause. "I should have handled it differently. There were other paths."

"You chose the most permanent one."

"Yes." She said it without flinching. "It was a failure of imagination as much as anything else. I had been operating in the same framework for so long that the response I chose was the one my framework provided." She looked at Mira directly. "I'm telling you this not to excuse it. I'm telling you because you've come a long way and you deserve a complete answer."

The garden sounds continued outside. The tea had gone cold on both sides of the table.

"The technique," Mira said. "Using the Bond to fold the casting through his own residue signature. You needed his license number for that."

"He gave me that, inadvertently, years ago. A legitimate Bond demonstration for one of my theory seminars. He was the volunteer caster. I read his signature then."

"And the selenite dust. The purchase through Petra Vane."

"She doesn't know what she bought it for. She thought she was running an errand." Oksana's voice was steady, but something shifted in it. "She is entirely uninvolved."

"I know. I spoke with Aldwick."

A brief silence. "You've been thorough."

"It's what I do."

Oksana looked at her for a long moment. The considering expression was back, sharpened now by something else: a precision that Mira recognized as the attention of a woman who had decided to say something she had been saving.

"Before you take this further," she said, "I want to ask you something. Not as a negotiation. As a genuine question."

"Ask," Mira said.

"You read the residue in the demonstration hall thirty years ago. The compressed-core structure. The point of origin at head height, four feet from the amplifier. You saw it and you filed 'slightly atypical' and you signed the report. Harlen Voss spent four weeks recovering and never received his license."

Mira said nothing.

"I'm not asking this to protect myself," Oksana said. "I'm asking because it seems relevant to understanding what you plan to do next. You signed that report. You have spent thirty years with what you knew, and what you did with what you knew. And now you are here, in my kitchen, with a residue comparison that is significant but not beyond dispute, deciding what to do with it." She looked at Mira with something that was not quite compassion but was adjacent to it. "I want to know how you understand the difference between what I did and what you did. Because I am not entirely sure I do."

This was, Mira had to acknowledge, a devastating question. It was devastating not because it was unfair but because it had a real answer, and the real answer was not simple.

"The difference," she said, "is that you knew what you were doing and chose it. At twenty-four, I was trying not to know. I was avoiding the knowledge." She paused. "That is not the same thing. But it is also not a comfortable distinction."

"No," Oksana said. "It's not."

"I'm going to amend the report," Mira said. "IR-34-071. I'm going to file a formal amendment with a corrected residue assessment. Whatever happens to you."

"That will be uncomfortable for you professionally."

"Yes."

"Your supervisor shaped that report. He's eighty-two. He's retired."

"I know."

"And you're still going to do it."

"Yes," Mira said. "Because thirty years ago I had the evidence in my lens and I wrote 'slightly atypical' and called it accurate. It wasn't accurate. Cornelius Veld deserved better than that, and so did Harlen Voss." She looked at Oksana steadily. "You could argue that I owe you this in some abstract sense, that my silence gave you thirty additional years. I don't accept that framing. I owe it to the record."

Oksana looked at her for a long time. The garden sounds persisted, small and certain, outside in the autumn afternoon.

"What are you going to do?" she said. "Now. With what you have."

"I'm going to go to the Inspector," Mira said. "And I'm going to tell him everything I've told you, except for the parts he already knows."

"He won't be able to compel a residue reading without a formal order."

"He won't need to. You've just confirmed the technique. You've confirmed the mechanism and the timing and the preparation. What I have from the lens is corroborating. It doesn't need to be the only evidence."

Oksana was quiet for a moment. Then she said, with the tone of someone who has made a decision at the end of a long road: "All right."

"All right?" Mira repeated.

"I've been doing this for nearly thirty years," Oksana said. "I've been very careful. I've been very good at it. And I made one mistake, with someone I trusted, and it has led here. I don't think I want to spend the remaining time I have trying to unpick this." She looked at the window. "I'm seventy-one. I'm tired of being careful. There is a certain relief," she said slowly, "in being done with it."

She reached across the table and took her cold tea and drank it as if it were warm, with the unhurried deliberateness of someone who has decided to be present in the moment she is in.

"I won't make your case easy for you," she said. "I'll have a solicitor, and the residue comparison is not perfect, and I'll use everything available to me. But I'm not going to run."

"I didn't think you would," Mira said.

She stood up, gathered her notebook, and put Prudence in her pocket. For a moment she stood in Oksana Rael's sitting room with its books, its theoretical papers, and its view of the alive garden. She thought about what it was to know something for nearly thirty years and to build a life around the knowing. What it had cost. What it had given.

She went out into the street and shut the door carefully behind her.

CHAPTER TWENTY

The Walk Back

She took the long way. The long way from Rael Street to the Inspector's office went by the market square and down through the commercial quarter and past Cooper Lane, which she had not planned but did not alter when she found herself walking it. It was a Friday afternoon in late autumn and the light was the color of old documents: amber at the edges, fading toward grey.

She walked slowly enough to think.

The market square at this hour on a Friday afternoon had the quality she associated with the end of working weeks: the stalls packing down with the efficiency of people who had been standing since six in the morning and were prepared to be done, the coffee cart doing its last trade of the day, the residue of the enchanted rain-gauge on the corner showing the faint blue signature of its weekly recalibration. A practitioner she didn't recognize was checking the weather-boards outside the cooperative office: young, Journeyman-level, moving with the careful attention of someone still learning the field work. She watched the Tier reading from a distance for a moment and found it correct and kept walking.

She had been looking away from things for thirty years. This was the conclusion she had been approaching for two weeks and had now arrived at fully, and it had the quality of a thing that is not a surprise but is still, when it arrives, large. She had looked away from the residue reading in the demonstration hall. She had looked away from the selenite dust in the ledger, filed it as a dot rather than a flag. She had looked away from what she knew on the morning she found Cornelius Veld, letting Brenn build his self-cast theory in peace. She had looked away from Haas's innocence until the investigation had moved far enough in the wrong direction that stopping it became an urgency. She had, in almost every moment when she had encountered something that required a decision she did not want to make, found a way to not quite make it.

This was not what she had told herself, for thirty years, about herself. She had told herself she was methodical. She had told herself she was professionally careful, that she did not act on incomplete information, that she waited until she had the full picture before committing to a position. These things were also true, and they were the language in which she had dressed the other thing, the more accurate thing, which was that she had been very skilled for a very long time at mistaking caution for cowardice.

She passed the front of Veld's Enchantments. The TEMPORARILY CLOSED sign was still in the window. She could see through the glass that someone had straightened the demonstration stand again and put a cloth over it. Delia's work, probably. She stood for a moment looking at the shop, thinking about Cornelius Veld. He had been careful, warm, and slightly jumpy, a man who wanted to understand the theory behind things. He had understood something, and he had been killed for understanding it. He had not deserved any of this. The shop had a specific quality now that she had been in and out of it half a dozen times: the quality of a place she had learned to read in the same way she read any space, through its residue and its organization and the specific story its surfaces told about the person who had occupied it. She had walked into it as an auditor and walked out of it as something she did not have a precise professional category for. A witness, maybe. A person with relevant information who had made decisions about when to share it and when to hold it and who was still living with those decisions.

She thought about Cornelius Veld's desk, which she had read with Prudence and found a defensive ward on the corner of, cast in his final hours by a man who knew something was coming and was trying to be prepared. He had been precise and careful until the very end. He had built the best ward he knew how to build and it had not been enough, because the person who cast the Severing Cascade had known exactly what the ward would look like and had designed the approach accordingly.

She stood looking at the TEMPORARILY CLOSED sign for a long moment.

Then she kept walking.

She thought about Harlen Voss, who was in his early fifties now and had never cast a spell since he was twenty years old.

She thought about Oksana Rael sitting in her sitting room with the books and the worktable and the alive garden, having said: I'm tired of being careful. There was something in this that she understood and did not want to understand. Being tired of it was not an excuse. It was also, she had to admit, something she recognized.

She thought about what it had cost her, thirty years of looking away. Not professionally: her career had been fine, her audits correct, her record clean. Personally. What it had cost in the small accounting of a life: the gap between what she knew and what she had done with what she knew, the slight perpetual discomfort of being a person who had signed a report she believed to be incomplete, the way this had sat in the grey archival box on the high shelf and generated a kind of low, constant pressure that she had learned to call something else.

She had, she thought, spent thirty years being a very good auditor in all the ways that were easy and a somewhat worse one in the one way that required something more than technical skill.

The way that required something more than technical skill was this: the willingness to put a finding on record that would make things difficult. Not difficult for others, which she had always been willing to do, but difficult for herself. She had spent three decades being genuinely excellent at noting what was uncomfortable about other people's work. She had been less willing to note what was uncomfortable about her own. This was, she supposed, the most ordinary kind of moral failure: not dramatic or violent or even particularly interesting. Just the daily practice of looking toward the edge of a thing and then, very slightly, looking away.

She was not going to do it again.

She stopped at a bench near the market square, because her feet had brought her there without being asked, and she sat down and took Prudence out of her coat pocket and held it in both hands. The lens caught the late afternoon light and threw it back in the amber that was its own color, the compound calcite and residue-sensitive mineral aggregate that had been warm in her hand for thirty-one years.

She looked at her own hands through the lens.

It was not a thing she did, usually. Auditors did not read their own residue: it was professionally unnecessary and personally strange, like reading your own handwriting in a mirror. But she raised Prudence and looked, and what she saw was what she had always known was there: her own license signature, Master Auditor, the layered history of thirty years of correct and careful work, the sediment of thousands of readings, thousands of assessments, thousands of renewal certificates countersigned and returned. It was, she thought, a good record. It was also not the whole record.

She lowered the lens and put it back in her pocket.

She got up from the bench.

Inspector Brenn's office was a ten-minute walk from the market square, through the administrative quarter, in a building she knew well. She had been there twice this month already. She had, both times, told him less than she knew.

Tonight she would tell him everything.

She thought about what everything meant: the residue comparison, the confirmation from Oksana's baseline, the conversation she had just had in the sitting room on Rael Street. Oksana had not confessed in any formal legal sense: she had answered questions and confirmed mechanisms and described her reasoning, and she had said she would not run. She had not explicitly said she had killed Cornelius Veld, in those words, but she had described the decision to act in a way that left no other interpretation. Whether this constituted a legally usable admission was for Brenn and the Guild's legal team to determine.

What Mira had was a residue comparison, a statement, a timeline, a procurement chain, and a conversation in which a retired Master-tier caster had discussed the mechanism and decision process of a murder with the equanimity of someone who had run out of reasons to maintain a story.

She also had IR-34-071 and the amendment she had promised to file. This was not Brenn's concern but the Guild's, and she would file it through the Guild's formal amendment process once the investigation was concluded. She had already drafted the corrected assessment. It was on her desk at home, written in her current hand, precise and accurate, with a note at the bottom explaining the delay in filing: that she had been twenty-four and had made a professional judgment that had not been correct, and that she was correcting it now.

She would sign this one too. She meant it.

The administrative quarter was quiet at this hour on a Friday: the offices closing, the last of the filing being completed, the formal machinery of governance winding down for the weekend and leaving the buildings to their stone and their paperwork. She had spent much of her professional life in buildings like these. She did not dislike them. They had the comfort of places that existed for a purpose and knew what it was.

She went up the steps to the Inspector's building and pushed open the front door.

A clerk at the reception desk looked up.

"I'd like to see Inspector Brenn," she said. "Tell him it's Mira Ashcroft from the Licensing Office. Tell him I have a full statement on the Veld matter."

The clerk sent a message. She sat in one of the chairs along the wall and held her notebook in her lap and waited.

She did not think about anything in particular while she waited. She noticed, as she usually noticed, the residue in the room: the faint accumulated signatures of the licensing officials who worked here, the neutral municipal residue of a building that processed a great deal of ordinary legal business. It was unremarkable. It was, in its way, comforting.

After seven minutes, Brenn came out himself rather than sending the clerk. He looked at her with the careful attention of a man who could see, from the quality of her stillness, that something had changed.

"Come in," he said.

She went in.

PART THREE

The Record

CHAPTER TWENTY-ONE

What Mira Tells the Inspector

Brenn's office had, at this hour, the quality of a room that had been working all day and was tired of it. The paper on his desk had shifted from organized to managed. The lamp was on against the early dark. He poured two cups of tea from a pot that had been sitting long enough to be strong, set one in front of her, and sat down, and she understood from the way he sat that he had told his staff to hold anything that wasn't urgent.

"Start where you need to start," he said.

She appreciated this more than she would have thought she would. She had been told, in various professional contexts, to take her time, to begin at the beginning, to start with the most recent events, to start with the earliest ones. None of those instructions had been as useful as this one, which recognized that the relevant beginning of this story was not a fixed point but a choice, and that it was hers to make.

She started with the visit to Oksana Rael that afternoon, because it was the freshest and the most direct. She described what she had found in the residue baseline: the Bond practice traces in the third layer, the specific offset timing consistent with repeated use of an inverted Bond technique, and the comparison to the partial second signature in her working notes from the morning she found Cornelius Veld. She described the conversation that had followed the reading.

She described it accurately, which meant she reported what Oksana had said and how she had said it and what she had confirmed by confirming it. She was not a lawyer and could not assess what was legally admissible; she was an auditor and she was reporting what she had observed with professional precision. Brenn wrote steadily throughout. He did not interrupt.

When she finished the account of the Oksana visit she placed her working notebook on the desk, open to the comparison notes and the timeline. She placed beside it the copy of Cornelius Veld's unsent letter, which she had carried for a week and a half. She placed beside that a summary sheet she had written at home that morning, before she posted the letter to Oksana, laying out the procurement chain from Oksana to Petra Vane to Aldwick to the selenite dust.

"That's the active evidence," she said. "There is also the historical matter, which is IR-34-071. I've already told you the report number. You'll need access to it." She paused. "I have a personal copy."

"I can request it through the Guild's sealed records office," Brenn said slowly, still writing. "Given the active investigation, I have grounds."

"You do. I would recommend doing that. The official copy may contain more than my personal one."

He looked up. "More in what sense?"

"My copy is the report as filed. The official sealed version may contain administrative annotations that were added after filing." She looked at the desk. "I am speculating. But a report that was actively shaped rather than simply completed would be the kind of document that generates internal correspondence, and internal correspondence sometimes ends up in the sealed file rather than the circulated copy."

Brenn was quiet for a moment. "You're telling me your supervisor suppressed your finding."

"I'm telling you my supervisor shaped the report, and that I complied with his shaping, and that he may have generated internal documentation about his own decision that neither of us has seen." She met his gaze. "I don't know what's in the sealed file. I'm telling you to look."

He looked at her for another moment and then wrote something down, and she could see from the angle of his pen that he was writing request sealed IR-34-071 official copy, annotated, and she felt something that was not quite relief and not quite dread but was in the territory between them.

He submitted the records request that evening. The sealed file arrived the next morning: Guild administrative procedure for a document relevant to an active homicide investigation was four hours, which Mira had not known and which meant the sealed file was on Brenn's desk by the time she arrived for a follow-up meeting at ten o'clock on Saturday morning.

She had not expected to see it in his hands when she came in. She had expected to give him the weekend to process. His expression told her he had not had a restful night.

"Sit down," he said. He did not pour tea this time. He opened the file on the desk and turned it toward her, and she looked at the document she had not seen before: the official annotated version, which was thicker than her personal copy by a considerable margin.

The additional material was in two sections. The first was Edwyn Foss's own internal correspondence, filed with his supervisor at the time: a memorandum, dated eleven days after the incident report, in which Foss noted that the junior auditor's on-site findings had contained observations "that could be read as inconsistent with the equipment malfunction determination" and recommending that the file be sealed to prevent "unnecessary speculation about a well-regarded member of the practitioner community." The memorandum had been approved and filed by his supervisor, whose countersignature was at the bottom in a hand she did not recognize.

Foss had known. He had not merely shaped the report under the pressure of an uncertain situation. He had assessed the junior auditor's findings, understood what they implied, and made a deliberate administrative decision to inter them where they could not be reached without clearance.

She read this for a long time without speaking. Then she turned to the second section of additional material.

The second section was not from Foss or the Guild. It was a single page on Inspector's office letterhead, dated four years after the incident, from a name she recognized: Inspector Daven Rook, who had trained the generation of Magical Crimes Officers that included Brenn's own training supervisor. The note was brief:

IR-34-071. Guild attributed to equipment malfunction. Residue assessment on file contains language ("slightly atypical," "within range of variation") that in my experience suggests observed anomalies were present but not recorded fully. Recommend independent review if case reopens. No further action at this time per Guild determination; file retained for reference.

Brenn said: "Rook was my training supervisor's mentor. I inherited his case notes as part of my practitioner archive when he retired." He looked at the desk. "He saw it. The Inspector's office saw it. The Guild's audit office saw it. And it was buried in four years of paperwork."

"Yes," Mira said.

"Rook recommended independent review."

"Yes."

"And nothing happened."

"Nothing happened," she said, "because the Guild determination was already on file and no one was willing to reopen it without a formal complaint, and no formal complaint was made because the only person who might have made one was a twenty-four-year-old junior auditor who had been strongly advised not to."

She had not intended this sentence to land the way it did. She had intended it as a factual account. Brenn looked at her with the expression of someone who was understanding something he had not understood before, and she looked back without managing her expression quite as well as she normally would.

"All right," he said, at last. He straightened the file. "I'm going to request the warrant."

"You have grounds."

"I have your residue reading, a circumstantial chain, and an informal statement from the suspect confirming the mechanism and her awareness that it was actionable. Yes, I have grounds." He was, she thought, talking through it as much for his own benefit as hers. "The residue comparison is the weak point. Your formal statement will be challenged."

"I know. The alternative to challenging it is a Guild Master-tier forensic review, which will take three weeks and the signature window will be largely closed. What Oksana said to me this afternoon is not challengeable, because she said it."

"It's not a formal confession."

"It is not," Mira agreed. "It is a retired Master-tier caster discussing the mechanism and decision process of a casting that killed a person, in response to questions about that specific casting, after being told that the residue reading had found evidence of Bond practice traces in her signature. In a court of law, that is for the Guild's legal team to assess. For the purposes of a warrant, it should be sufficient."

Brenn sat with this for a long moment. She watched him doing the calculation that she had already done, which was: is the case good enough, and what does pursuing it cost, and what does not pursuing it cost. She had spent three weeks in this calculation. He had forty-five minutes.

He looked at the Rook note. He looked at the Foss memorandum. He looked at his own case file and the formal statement she had submitted four days ago. He picked up his pen.

She watched him read the Rook note a second time, which was a different reading from the first: the first had been comprehension, this one was assessment. Rook had seen it. An Inspector from a previous generation had looked at the same file Mira had looked at and had written down, in plain professional language, that he believed something had been covered and that the case should be reopened if the opportunity arose. And then the opportunity had not arisen. The Guild's determination was on file, the case was closed, and Rook had retired. His case notes had passed to his successor, and eventually to the person sitting across from Mira now, who was thirty-three, was very good at his job, and had not been born when the incident happened.

She thought about what it meant that Rook had seen it. That Foss had known, and documented his own knowledge, and that the documentation had been sealed with the file. That a chain of people had held pieces of this and done nothing with the pieces, not because they were negligent but because they had each encountered a version of the same calculation: the Guild's determination was on file. The cost of challenging it was high. The available evidence was circumstantial. The window in which action was possible had already closed. The window was open again now. It had been opened by a careful man who wanted to understand the theory behind things and had been killed for the understanding.

"I'll have the warrant by Monday morning," he said. "You should be at the office when we serve it. Not because you need to be there, but because you've been in this longer than anyone and I'd rather have a Master-tier lens on the scene."

"I'll be there," she said.

She walked home in the early evening of a Saturday, two days before the arrest. She passed the market square, which was doing what it did on Saturday evenings: the tail end of the day stalls, the beginning of the dinner-hour foot traffic, the familiar Thornhallow sound of a town settling into its weekend. The lamp above the Licensing Office was off; it was a Saturday and the office was closed. She had a key. She did not go in.

She went home and fed the provisional cat and sat at the kitchen table and thought about Edwyn Foss, who had been eighty-two for two years and was, by all accounts, a man with a comfortable retirement and a garden and occasional visits from his grandchildren. She thought about what it meant to know what he had done, and to have known for thirty-one years that she had complied with it, and to have the documentation of it in her possession for the first time.

She thought about it for a long time.

Then she took out her Guild notepaper and began drafting the amendment to IR-34-071. She had already written it twice in the past week, but she had not considered it final. She considered the version she wrote now, at her kitchen table on Saturday evening, to be the version she would sign.

She wrote it in the language of a professional report, which was the only language available to her for this purpose and which was, she decided, adequate. Professional language was not cold. It was precise. Precision was not the same as indifference. She had spent thirty-one years in the imprecision of "slightly atypical" and she knew exactly what it had cost and she was not going to write another word of it.

The amendment stated, in the clear, specific terms of a corrected residue assessment, that the compressed-core structure of the cascade residue in the demonstration hall had originated from a point in space inconsistent with the amplifier housing, at head height, in the direction of the senior observer's position. It stated that this pattern was, in the assessing auditor's professional opinion at the time of the original assessment, *significantly* atypical rather than slightly so. It stated that the original assessment had not fully reflected these observations. It gave the report number, the date of the original assessment, the name of the assessing auditor, and the reason for the amendment: *correction of an incomplete finding.*

She signed it.

She meant it.

CHAPTER TWENTY-TWO

The Ward Pattern

The warrant was served on Monday morning at nine o'clock, which was, Brenn had explained to her, the conventional hour for this kind of thing in Thornhallow: early enough to be efficient, late enough to be decent. The Guild's provincial enforcement officer came with him, as the arrest involved a licensed Master-tier practitioner and required a licensed witness of equivalent standing. Mira came as the auditor of record, which was the professional designation Brenn had arranged for her, and which was accurate and also the only way he could formally justify her presence.

It was a grey Monday, which was appropriate. Autumn at its most October.

Oksana opened the door herself, as she always did. She was dressed, which meant she had been expecting them, which meant she had understood on Friday afternoon that the conversation on Friday afternoon was not the end of anything. She looked at Brenn, then at the enforcement officer beside him, then at Mira slightly behind them. Her expression was composed in the way that she had been composed throughout: not blank, not performed, but the genuine steadiness of a person who had made a decision and was living in it.

"Inspector," she said. "Come in."

They came in. The sitting room had the same books, the same worktable, the same view of the alive garden. The residue observation journal was closed. The pre-standardization compendium was on the shelf where it always was.

Brenn delivered the formal caution in the Guild's precise language, which was designed to be impossible to misunderstand: she was being detained on suspicion of unlicensed casting resulting in death, specifically the use of an Archived formulation, the Severing Cascade, in conjunction with an improperly applied Amplification Bond, resulting in the death of Cornelius Veld, licensed Tier 3 Practitioner. The enforcement officer noted the time. Oksana listened without interrupting.

When Brenn finished she said: "May I see the evidence summary?"

Brenn had brought it. He had discussed this with Mira on Sunday: whether to bring the summary or to hold it for the formal proceedings, and Mira had said that Oksana had asked to see the evidence on Friday and had said she would use everything available to her, and a woman who had operated as carefully as she had for nearly thirty years deserved to see what had been found. Brenn had agreed.

Oksana read the summary at her own pace. It was four pages. She read it twice, which Mira recognized as a thorough reading rather than a rereading: the first pass to understand the structure, the second to assess the specific claims. Her expression did not change significantly. She set the pages down on the worktable.

"The residue comparison is the weakest point," she said. It was not said provocatively. It was an accurate assessment.

"Yes," Brenn said.

"My solicitor will challenge it."

"That is your right."

She nodded. Then she looked at the summary pages again, and Mira watched her find the section she was looking for, which was the entry about the ward pattern on Cornelius Veld's desk. It was the last piece of evidence in the summary, listed under the heading Corroborating Physical Evidence.

The entry read:

A personal defensive ward of recent casting was found on the right-front corner of the deceased's work desk. The ward employs a compressed-core construction with upper secondary reinforcement, a teaching-specific architectural style associated with the pre-standardization provincial training tradition and documented in the Guild's historical methodology records as characteristic of a specific pedagogical lineage active from approximately 45 years ago. The Severing Cascade, as cast, displays counter-shaping in its approach geometry that is consistent with the caster having anticipated this specific defensive structure. The counter-shaping would require prior knowledge of the ward pattern's architecture. The deceased's documented instructor in private theory (Oksana Rael, Master-tier, licensed) is identified in the Guild's teaching credit records as the practitioner associated with this pedagogical tradition.

Oksana read this, and she was very still for a moment, and Mira understood what the stillness meant: it was the stillness of someone who had underestimated one thing. She had known, when she cast the Severing Cascade, that Cornelius Veld would raise a ward in his final seconds. She had counter-shaped the casting around it with the instinctive precision of a teacher who knew exactly what her student's defensive ward looked like, because she had taught him to build it. She had not considered, until this moment, that the counter-shaping itself would be readable. That it would constitute evidence of a knowledge no one else could have possessed.

She set the papers down.

She was, Mira could see, doing what she had been doing since the reading: the precise accounting of what had been found, what it would take to challenge it, and what space remained for challenge. The residue comparison was the weakest point, as she had immediately identified. But the ward pattern entry was different. The ward pattern entry connected two things that should not have been connected: the method of the killing and the specific knowledge required to kill that particular person in that particular way. A caster who had never taught Cornelius Veld could not have known the precise shape of the ward he would raise in his final seconds. The counter-shaping was not a generic application. It was personal, and it was precise, and it had required knowing not just that a ward would be raised but what that ward would look like.

Thirty-five years of teaching had a shape, and the shape was visible, and she had built the counter to it out of the same knowledge she had used to build the original.

"He cast it," she said, quietly. "The ward. He had time to try." She paused. "He was always quick."

"He was," Mira said.

A silence in the room. The garden sounds, just audible.

Oksana looked at her directly. "You said you would amend the original report."

"I have drafted the amendment. I'll file it through the formal process this week."

"Will it be accepted?"

"The Guild's amendment process is straightforward for a corrected finding from the assessing auditor. There is no mechanism to refuse it." She paused. "There may be professional consequences for me. That is not your concern."

"No," Oksana said. "But I asked anyway." She looked at the enforcement officer, who had been standing quietly near the door. "I'm ready."

The process that followed was, in the way of these things, more administrative than dramatic. Oksana's solicitor was contacted. A Guild legal representative was called. The formal transfer of custody was documented in triplicate, which was the Guild's requirement for the arrest of a Master-tier licensed practitioner, and Mira countersigned the documentation in her capacity as auditor of record. The enforcement officer was professional and quiet throughout. Oksana was professional and quiet throughout.

She took her coat from the hook near the door. She paused with one hand on the door frame and looked back at the sitting room: the books, the worktable, the garden window. A long look, and then she went out.

The enforcement officer held the door. Brenn stood aside with the quality of a person who was doing something significant and had found a way to do it with dignity. Mira stood near the window with her completed documentation and watched. Oksana Rael crossed the sitting room for the last time with the posture she had always had and would apparently always have: the posture of someone who had decided, at some point in her twenties, how she was going to occupy a room, and had never reconsidered. She did not look at the worktable. She did not look at the books. She looked at the garden window, which showed the grey November sky above the wall, and then she went through the door, and the garden sounds continued without her.

Mira stayed to complete the documentation while Brenn accompanied Oksana and the enforcement officer. When she was done she stood in Oksana's sitting room for a moment in the absence of a space that has just been left. She did not look at the worktable. She looked at the garden.

Petter Haas was released from the Inspector's holding facility on Monday afternoon, four hours after the arrest. His fraud charges remained active. He walked out of the facility and called his solicitor and did not speak to anyone from the Licensing Office. This was appropriate.

Mira did not go to the shop on Monday. She went home, and she completed the formal documentation for the audit of record, and she filed it through the office's administrative system. She drafted a formal notification to the Guild's enforcement division regarding the licensing fraud case against Haas, which was now Brenn's active file and no longer hers to manage. She drafted a closing note to Delia Veld regarding the estate audit. She was efficient and thorough, and did not think about anything in particular while she was working.

She thought about it at dinner.

On Tuesday she came back through Cooper Lane on her lunch walk, which was not the most direct route from anything to anything but was the route she took. The TEMPORARILY CLOSED sign was still in the window of Veld's Enchantments. But someone had replaced the cloth over the demonstration stand with the proper display cover, the burgundy one with the shop's name embroidered in the corner, and the display cases had been cleaned. She could see through the glass that the ledger was on the counter, open.

Delia, she thought, had made her decision.

She stood for a moment looking at the shop front and thought about Cornelius Veld, who had been careful and warm, and who had wanted to understand the theory behind things. She thought about Harlen Voss, who was fifty-one years old and ran, she had found in the Guild's records, a plant nursery in the eastern province. She thought about Tam Finch, nineteen, who had taken a letter off a dead man's desk because he loved him and did not know what else to do.

She walked back to the Licensing Office and did her afternoon's work and went home and fed the provisional cat.

It was a correct afternoon.

CHAPTER TWENTY-THREE

The Amendment

The formal amendment process for a sealed Guild incident report required three documents: the corrected assessment itself, signed by the original assessing officer; a covering statement explaining the reason for the amendment and the nature of the correction; and a notification request form directing the Guild's administrative office to inform all parties of record of the amendment and to update the Archive accordingly.

Mira had completed all three by Wednesday. She submitted them through the Guild's regional office, hand-delivered, because this was not the kind of paperwork she was going to trust to the post. The regional administrator, a man named Prewett whom she had worked with for twelve years, accepted the documents with the neutral efficiency that the Guild's administrative staff deployed when handling something they recognized as significant but were not certain how to categorize. He gave her a receipt and a reference number and said the processing time was five to eight working days.

"The parties of record notification," she said. "Who is listed?"

He checked the file. "The original investigating officer, listed as Senior Auditor Edwyn Foss, retired. The three persons named in the incident report. The Guild's Archival Division, as the holder of the sealed file." He paused. "And the provincial enforcement office, given the active homicide investigation."

"Thank you," she said.

She walked home from the regional office through the market square, which was doing its Wednesday morning business in the fine indifference of a market square in late autumn. She thought about Edwyn Foss, who would receive a formal Guild notification informing him that an amendment had been filed to a report he had written thirty-one years ago. He would not, at eighty-two, be legally accountable for what the Foss memorandum revealed about his conduct. The statute of limitations on administrative misconduct of this type was fifteen years. She had checked.

This was, she acknowledged to herself, a fact that she found neither fully satisfying nor fully unsatisfying. He had been a kind man who had made an institutional calculation and had buried thirty-one years of consequences under a filing code. He was eighty-two. She was fifty-four. She had made her own institutional calculation at twenty-four. The difference between their calculations was that his had been deliberate and hers had been compliant, and the difference between deliberate and compliant was real and also somewhat uncomfortable to sit with as a source of self-justification. She sat with it anyway.

She did not call him.

The notification was the Guild's job. She had done her job.

The notification to Harlen Voss was the one she found herself thinking about most. He was fifty-one. He had not been a practitioner for thirty-one years and would never be one. The amendment would not restore his residue pathways, which had been damaged in the Severing Cascade and which could not be repaired. It would, she hoped, give him something accurate: an official record that what had happened to him was not an equipment malfunction, that it had been deliberate, and that the Guild had known this and had not told him. This was a very small thing to give a person who had lost the profession they had trained for. It was the only thing currently available.

She had written a separate, personal letter to Harlen Voss, which she had sent directly to his address in the eastern province three days ago. The letter was brief. It told him who she was, what she had found, and what the amendment would say. It told him she had been the junior auditor who signed the original assessment, and that her assessment had not been complete. It told him she was sorry for this. It told him the Guild's victim services division could be contacted at the following address if he wished to pursue any formal matter arising from the amended finding.

She had not expected a reply quickly. She had not expected one at all, possibly. What she received on Thursday morning was a single sentence on a plain card:

Thank you for telling me the truth. I had always suspected something. H.V.

She read the card twice and put it in the desk drawer and sat for a moment with the drawer still open, which was not something she normally did. She had a habit of completing actions: opening things, reading them, filing them, moving on. The half-open drawer was an anomaly. She looked at the card through the gap.

I had always suspected something. This was a sentence that could mean many things. It could mean that Harlen Voss had spent thirty years with a background awareness that his injury had not been accidental, and had simply learned to live alongside that awareness without the evidence to act on it, which was its own kind of looking-away. Or it could mean that he had made peace with the uncertainty and the notification was simply a confirmation of something he had filed and released. She did not know which. She was not going to know which. The card was what she had.

She closed the drawer. She went back to the morning's files.

That afternoon she walked past the Guild's recalibration facility on her way home, not because it was on her route but because she wanted to see it. The facility occupied a ground-floor room in the Guild's provincial office building: a small room with specialized equipment and a residue-controlled environment and a technician she had worked with for nine years. Prudence had been delivered on Monday morning. She would collect it on Friday. The technician had confirmed this in his methodical way, with the same care he brought to all precision work.

She stood outside the building for a moment. She did not go in. There was nothing to go in for, and the technician would call when it was ready.

She went home and fed the provisional cat and did not think about what it meant to be without the lens that had been in her pocket or her hand for thirty-one years. She was very good at not thinking about things.

Prudence went in for recalibration on Tuesday, which was the correct interval following a major investigative use: the lens was sensitive enough that extended high-detail reading could introduce micro-alignments in the calcite compound, and the Guild required recalibration after any deployment involving Bond-level residue analysis. Mira had submitted the lens the morning after the arrest. The recalibration took five days.

She had not been without Prudence for five consecutive days in twelve years. She was aware of this in the specific way she was aware of the absence of things she used habitually: not exactly discomfort, but a kind of ambient wrongness, the way a room feels slightly different when a piece of furniture has been moved. She did her ordinary audit work with the office's standard Journeyman-model lens, which she used for routine renewal checks and which was adequate for the purpose. It was not Prudence.

On Thursday Bram took her to lunch. This was the standing appointment, restored to its usual schedule after the weeks of irregularity, and they walked to the small café around the corner from the office in the early November cold and ordered the daily plate, which was a lamb pie, and Bram put both hands around his cup of tea and said: "Tell me."

She told him.

She had given him pieces of it over the past three weeks, enough for him to understand the general shape of what had happened, but she had not given him the full account. She gave it to him now, in order, starting from the Friday morning she found Cornelius Veld on his shop floor and ending with the amendment she had submitted on Wednesday. She gave him the selenite dust and the incident report and the compressed-core ward and the letter on the desk and Oksana in her sitting room saying she was tired of being careful.

She gave him her own part in it: the twenty-four-year-old signature, the thirty-one years of the grey archival box, the morning she stood in Veld's shop with a Severing Cascade in her lens and let Brenn build a different theory. She gave him all of it because he was the person she worked with and because the standing Thursday lunch was specifically the appointment at which they reviewed the week's work and because she had been sitting across from him for three weeks with a very large part of the week's work undisclosed, and she was done with that.

Bram listened. He was very good at listening, in the

way

of a person who was genuinely interested in what you were saying and was not organizing his response while you said it but was simply receiving it. When she finished he was quiet for a moment, eating his pie.

"The lens," he said at last. "When you read the residue in the shop. Before you called it in."

"Yes."

"You knew immediately."

"Immediately, yes."

He nodded slowly. "And then you called the Inspector."

"I called the Inspector."

"And then you spent three weeks," he said, not quite a question, "being very professionally thorough." He looked at his tea. "I wondered what the look was, but I thought it wasn't my place to ask before you were ready."

"It wasn't your place to ask," she agreed. "And I appreciate that you didn't."

"I brought soup."

"You brought soup," she said, "which was the correct thing to do."

They ate in companionable silence for a moment. Outside the café window the street was doing its Thursday business: the licensing office two buildings down, the tea shop across from it, the cloud of pigeons outside the grain merchant's that was a permanent feature of the district regardless of season.

"Are you all right?" Bram asked. Not as a pleasantry. As a question.

She considered it with the precision she brought to questions that deserved precision. "I will be," she said. "The amendment is filed. The investigation is Brenn's. The audit files for the week are current. I am going to collect Prudence on

Monday and conduct the Finch Textiles audit on Tuesday and then I will be all right."

"Good," he said. He reached for the bread basket. "Do you want the Merchant Quarter walk-through next Thursday, or shall I do it?"

He ate for a moment in the companionable way he ate when he was thinking about something and had decided not to rush toward it. Outside the cafe window the licensing office was visible between the buildings: the brass plate catching the thin November light.

"Can I ask you something," he said, "that isn't really my business."

"You can ask."

"When you signed it. The original report. At twenty-four." He looked at his tea. "Did you know, in the moment, that it wasn't right?"

She had not expected this question. Not because it was indelicate. Bram was never indelicate. It was because the question was specific, and specific meant he had been thinking about it carefully, which meant he understood that the general shape of the story she had just told was not the most important thing about it.

"Yes," she said.

He nodded slowly.

"I knew," she said, "and I had a supervisor who offered me a way to not quite know. And I took the way he offered. And then I was twenty-four, and twenty-five, and the door was closed." She looked at the window. "It's not a dramatic failure. That's almost the worst part of it. It's just the smallest possible version of the thing: a junior person who wanted to belong to an institution, and a senior person who made the cost of belonging very clear, and a choice that was made in thirty seconds and then lived in for thirty years."

Bram was quiet for a moment. Then he said: "And the amendment."
"Filed on Wednesday."
"And the statement to the Inspector."
"Also on file."
He picked up his cup and looked at it. "Good," he said. Not with relief, which was what she might have expected, but with a specific steadiness that she recognized as the way Bram Wester said things he had concluded: fully, without room for revision. "I've worked with you for seven years," he said, "and I've always thought you were the best auditor I'd ever seen and occasionally one of the most difficult people to have lunch with." He set down the cup. "I'm glad you told me."
"I should have told you sooner," she said.
"You told me now," he said. "That's the part that counts."

"You do it," she said. "I'll take the Eastgate renewals."

"Perfect," he said, with the cheerfulness of a man who had just been confirmed in his preference, and they finished their lunch in the way they had been finishing their Thursday lunches for seven years: efficiently, pleasantly, and with a shared understanding of what the next week needed to look like.

She went home that evening and found, on her doorstep, the provisional cat sitting beside a small potted plant. The plant was a winter-flowering sage, in a terracotta pot with a note tucked into the soil:

For the person who handled things. D.V.

She brought it inside and put it on the kitchen windowsill, which was where it would get the most light, and fed the cat, and thought that Delia Veld was the sort of person who sent exactly the right thing.

CHAPTER TWENTY-FOUR

Delia Opens the Shop

Three weeks after the arrest, on a Tuesday in the third week of November, Veld's Enchantments reopened.

The license transfer had been processed by the Licensing Office: straightforward succession, Delia Veld taking the commercial license in her own name, Tier 3 provisional pending her first full-year audit, with the existing equipment registry transferred and updated. The documentation had required six forms, two witnessed signatures, and a fee that Delia had paid without comment. Mira had countersigned the provisional certificate personally, which was within her authority as the provincial senior auditor, and had done so with a completeness of attention that she would have given to any significant transfer.

She went to the shop on Tuesday morning, ostensibly to deliver the final estate audit report, which was ready and which she could have sent. She had, she acknowledged to herself as she walked down Cooper Lane, been finding legitimate reasons to check on the shop for several days. This was not entirely professional. She accepted it.

The window display had been rearranged. The self-warming bed bricks were still there, along with the weather-sealed window frames, but Delia had moved them to the back of the display. She had put three new items in the front: a small device that apparently self-organized a writing desk, a compact residence-warming unit in a style more contemporary than anything Cornelius had stocked, and a demonstration card that read UNDER NEW MANAGEMENT, SAME CARE in a clean, plain typeface. The typeface was not quite the Guild standard, and was slightly better-looking for it.

The door was unlocked. The bell rang.

Tam Finch was behind the counter. He had a different coat, not his training coat but a work apron over his ordinary clothes, which was what shop staff wore. He looked at Mira with the expression of someone who had been expecting her and was somewhat relieved she had arrived.

"She's in the back," he said. "She said to send you through."

The back workroom had been reorganized. The casting workbench was in the same position, but the component shelves had been relabeled in a different hand and the ventilation system had been adjusted: Mira could feel the slightly improved airflow. Delia was at the bench, working over the inventory ledger with a set of colored markers that were familiar from the estate audit two weeks ago. She had the same work coat, the same focused quality of someone who was exactly where they had decided to be.

"Miss Ashcroft." She set the markers down. "Is the paperwork correct?"

"Entirely." Mira placed the estate audit report on the clear end of the bench. "Everything is in order. The provisional certificate is valid until the first full audit, which will be in twelve months."

"I know." Delia looked at the report. "I've read the provisional requirements. I'm within my Tier on everything currently in the shop. Tam is keeping his apprentice registration active through the training center. The Haas partnership is dissolved, as of last week, formally." She said "formally" in a tone that suggested informally it had been dissolved some time before.

"The Haas fraud case," Mira said. "The Inspector's office is handling it separately. It should have no bearing on the shop's standing."

"Good." She looked up. "I know what it cost you. The investigation."

"It was my job," Mira said, which was true and also slightly incomplete. Delia gave her the look of someone who could tell the difference.

"My father," Delia said, "spent the last weeks of his life frightened, and trying not to show me, and working through something on his own because that was the kind of person he was. He found something that mattered and he tried to do something about it." She straightened the estate audit report without looking at it. "I'd like to know what he found. The full account. If you're willing."

Mira sat down on the workroom's spare stool and told her.

She gave her the complete version: Oksana's teaching, the incident thirty-one years ago, the conversation Cornelius had apparently had with Oksana in which Oksana said something that revealed, to a careful listener, what she had done. She gave her the letter and the selenite dust and the residue reading. She gave her the amendment and what it said and what it would mean for the official record.

She gave her, as carefully as she could, the account of her own part: that she had been in the room thirty-one years ago, that she had seen something she had not fully reported, that the case might have been resolved before it reached Cornelius Veld if she had been braver at twenty-four. She did not say this as a performance of guilt. She said it because Delia was entitled to know the full picture and the full picture included this.

Delia listened with the stillness she had shown at the memorial and at the estate audit: not blank, not cold, but the attention of someone who was taking in information they needed. When Mira finished she was quiet for a moment.

"He would have found it anyway," Delia said at last. "Whatever was in that report or not, he would have found the thing he needed to find. He was that kind of person." She looked at the wall. "Oksana was the person he trusted most outside of family. When he began to understand what she was, it would have been like that." She did not specify like what. She did not need to.

"He tried to do the right thing," Mira said.

"He always tried to do the right thing," Delia said, and there was thirty-five years of loving a careful, methodical, warm, slightly anxious man in the sentence, and Mira let it be there.

They were quiet for a moment. Through the door they could hear Tam in the front of the shop: the careful movements of a young person learning where things went, the occasional small sound of a jar or a box being placed, assessed, and placed again.

"Are you thinking about retirement?" Delia asked. It was said in the blunt, sideways manner of Delia's conversation: not a challenge, not a pleasantry, but a real question asked at an unexpected angle.

"I am fifty-four," Mira said.

"That's not an answer."

"No," she agreed. "I'm not thinking about retirement. I'm thinking about the Eastgate renewals next Thursday and a textile studio audit next week that has been on my schedule for a month, and what I'm going to do about the fact that my neighbor's cat has apparently decided she lives with me now." She paused. "Retirement seems premature."

"Good," Delia said. "The province needs someone who actually knows what they're looking at."

Mira accepted it. She gathered her things.

There was a thing she had not said in the course of the conversation, which was that Cornelius Veld's immaculate files had made her job both easier and harder. Easier because the documentation of his work was complete and the estate audit was straightforward. Harder because thoroughness was its own kind of argument: a man who kept records this carefully had expected to be accountable to them for a long time. He had not expected to stop.

She did not say this. She gathered her case and stood up and looked at the organized back workroom of the shop that Delia Veld had decided to keep, and thought that the decision to keep it was its own form of the same argument.

This was, Mira thought, one of the more satisfying professional assessments she had received in her career, and it came from a woman in her late twenties who had been running her father's shop for a week. She accepted it.

She was gathering her things to leave when it happened. A sound from the front: a small crash, then a brief intake of breath, then nothing. Mira went to the workroom doorway.

Tam Finch was behind the counter. He had a jar of calibration dust in one hand that he had clearly just caught: his arm was extended at an awkward angle, slightly too fast for a purely physical catch, and there was a faint residue shimmer around his wrist that faded in the second she was watching it. A low-Tier instinctive casting, the kind that happened before the mind caught up. The kind that meant something specific about what was developing in his practitioner pathways.

He looked at Mira. His expression was the expression of someone who had done something in front of an auditor that was, technically, within his apprentice registration but was also a casting that had not been registered in advance.

Mira looked at him for one moment.

"The shelf second from the left," she said. "The calibration dust goes behind the color standards, not in front. The light gets at it otherwise."

"Right," he said. "Yes. Thank you."

She gathered her things and went out.

She walked back to the Licensing Office in the November cold, which was the proper cold now, winter-adjacent and certain of itself. She thought about Tam Finch, nineteen, who had instincts that were beginning to be faster than his understanding of them. She thought about what a very good junior auditor he might make, in four or five years, when his training was complete and his instincts were trained and he had learned to look at things in the way that you learned to look at things when looking at them was your profession.

She thought about the fact that she was fifty-four and not yet done.

CHAPTER TWENTY-FIVE

An Irregular Casting

Prudence came back on Monday, as promised, and was slightly wrong in the grip.

This was expected: recalibration involved a full disassembly of the calcite compound, the brass housing, and the pressure-adjusted focusing ring. When the components were reassembled the tolerances were set fresh, which meant the lens was precisely what it was supposed to be, and not precisely what it had been. In five or six weeks the grip would wear back to something close to familiar. For now it sat in her palm at an angle approximately three degrees off from where it had lived for thirty-one years, and she was aware of this every time she picked it up.

She picked it up on Tuesday morning, put it in her coat pocket beside the day's audit forms, and walked to the east side.

Finch and Wester Textile Enchantments occupied a building on the far side of the Eastgate district, past the warehouses, the commercial laundry, and the small industries that the eastern quarter had always specialized in: the work that required space, ventilation, and neighbors who didn't object to the occasional smell of hot metal or dye. It was not a district Mira visited often. The east-side businesses operated at Tier 1 and Tier 2 mostly, and their audit cycles were long and their paperwork generally adequate.

The sign outside the studio read FINCH AND WESTER TEXTILE ENCHANTMENTS, LICENSED TIER 2, with the Guild seal in the corner and the hours in plain type. A second, smaller sign read CUSTOM WORK BY APPOINTMENT. The window displayed a length of cloth that shifted color very slightly as the light changed: a weather-response enchantment, popular in outer garments and legitimately within Tier 2 range. It was well-executed. The shift was smooth and the color range was tasteful.

She tried the door. Unlocked. The bell above it rang.

The interior was larger than it looked from the street: a showroom at the front, with bolts of fabric on standing racks and a demonstration counter, and behind it, visible through an open doorway, the workshop proper. The smell was of hot brass, lanolin, and something slightly mineral, the working-space residue smell she had been breathing for thirty-one years. Three casting looms stood along the west wall, each one the size of a writing desk: specialized enchantment equipment designed to apply casting residue evenly across textile fibers. Two of the three were in operation, the residue shimmer visible even without the lens.

A woman of about sixty came through from the workshop, removing her work gloves. This would be either Finch or Wester: the registration listed two proprietors, neither of whom was related to Tam, despite the name. She had the compact efficiency of someone who had been making things for a long time and had the hands to show for it.

"Miss Ashcroft, yes?" She had a slight northern accent. "I had your colleague's notice last month. We're a bit behind on the renewal, I know. Bram said it wasn't urgent."

"It isn't," Mira said. "I'm here for the inspection, not to levy a penalty. Shall we start with the equipment?"

They started with the equipment. The two looms in operation and the third at rest, plus a hem-finishing press and a sizing bath and two smaller portable enchantment applicators that were listed in the supplemental register. She went through them methodically, and Prudence was slightly wrong in the grip throughout, and she held it steadily and read what it showed her.

The first loom: Tier 2, registration number consistent with the license, a color-response enchantment in the middle of its indicated range, running evenly. Clean residue, no Bond signatures, no Tier overstep. The caster's signature was the northerner's: a tidy, experienced Tier 2 pattern with the density of someone who had been casting at this level for twenty years and was very good at it.

The second loom: same pattern, different enchantment, a warmth-retention application for winter-weight fabrics. Also Tier 2, also clean, also within license. The residue was fresher on this one, meaning it had been cast more recently, which was consistent with the seasonal shift toward heavier fabric work.

The third loom, at rest: a light-reflection enchantment half-applied, paused mid-work. This one she read more carefully, because half-completed work was where irregularities sometimes lived. She read it from the top of the application to the midpoint where it had stopped, and it was Tier 2 throughout, clean throughout, with the same caster signature and no sign of any technique she had not expected to find.

She lowered Prudence and made her notes in the precise, specific language of a professional audit: loom one, Tier 2 certified, registration number cross-referenced, residue clean. Loom two, the same. Loom three, the same, with a note that the half-completed application should be completed before the counter was refilled, as incomplete applications could create residue density anomalies if left in mid-state for more than a week.

The proprietor, whose name was Ines Wester and who had been running the textile studio for fourteen years and had an excellent instinct for when an auditor was finding something and when they weren't, visibly relaxed at this last note. "It'll be done today," she said.

"No urgency." Mira made the final notation and moved to the smaller equipment.

The portable applicators were clean. The hem-finishing press had a small residue irregularity on the press plate: not a violation, but the faintest edge of Tier 2 energy running slightly hotter than the registered range, consistent with a press plate that needed its calibration checked. She noted it.

"Serviced?" she asked.

"Last spring," Ines Wester said, with the look of someone doing rapid mental arithmetic. "I'll get it in before the end of the quarter."

"Good. It's not in violation. It's a maintenance flag."

She finished the equipment inspection and moved to the documents: the registration files, the annual renewal forms, the commission records for the past year. Everything was present and most of it was organized and the parts that were not organized were organized enough to be verified without significant effort. She worked through it in the systematic way she worked through all documentation: not faster when it looked clean, not slower when it looked complicated, simply steady and complete.

An hour and twenty minutes after she had arrived, she was done.

She sat at the demonstration counter with the renewal forms in front of her and wrote her conclusions in the boxes designed for them: equipment in compliance, documentation current, one maintenance flag for the press plate, no violations, renewal recommended. She wrote the date and her reference number and her professional designation.

She picked up her pen.

She thought, for a moment, about a junior auditor who had been twenty-four years old and had written "slightly atypical" when she meant something else entirely, and who had carried that for thirty-one years in a grey archival box on a high shelf. She thought about the version of herself who had signed that report, and the version who had signed the amended one last week, and what the distance between them had cost and what it had taken to cross it.

She thought about Cornelius Veld's immaculate paperwork, and the selenite dust in the ledger, and the way he had looked at his street on the last day of his life.

She thought about Prudence, slightly wrong in the grip, which would wear back to familiar in five or six weeks.

She signed the renewal form.

She put the pen down.

In thirty-one years she had countersigned approximately four thousand renewal certificates, which was the kind of number that accumulated without being noticed and then, when noticed, became briefly vertiginous. Four thousand correct mornings. Four thousand pieces of documentation that said: this practitioner is licensed, this equipment is registered, this casting is within its authorized Tier. Four thousand small guarantees that the system was working as it was supposed to work.

She had believed in this work from the first day she did it, and she believed in it still. The belief had not been shaken by what she had found in Cornelius Veld's residue or in the grey archival box or in the sealed Guild file or in Oksana Rael's sitting room. If anything, the belief was clearer now than it had been in a long time, because she had spent three weeks understanding in precise detail what happened when someone decided that the rules were for other people and the knowledge was for the select and the inconvenient could be made to stop. The rules were for everyone. The knowledge was part of the record. The inconvenient, in her experience, usually had the most to say.

Ines Wester was waiting near the door with the polite impatience of someone who had a press plate to finish calibrating.

Mira gathered her things.

She meant it.

Ines Wester walked her out, and the Tuesday morning was cold and clear, and the east side was going about its working business in the precise and ordinary way of a district that made things and did not think about making them as remarkable. She walked back through the Eastgate and through the commercial quarter and through the market square, which smelled of bread and damp stone and the sharp edge of winter coming.

The brass plate above the Licensing Office door caught the light as she turned onto the office street:

THORNHALLOW PROVINCIAL LICENSING OFFICE,
ROYAL GUILD OF LICENSED PRACTITIONERS,
AUTHORIZED AUDIT AND RENEWAL STATION.

Below it, in smaller text, the operational hours and the Guild seal.

She had walked under that plate approximately two thousand and seventeen times. She looked up at it.

Then she went in.

www.ingramcontent.com/pod-product-compliance
Lightning Source LLC
LaVergne TN
LVHW010658110826
845149LV00014B/3149